It would be a pity
to break the pattern

"Don't you realize," Lynn went on, "that every time we've met you've found reason to be annoyed with me?"

Blair's expression was amused as he reminded her mockingly, "I seem to recall a few moments yesterday when my annoyance appeared to have evaporated slightly."

Lynn found it difficult to meet his eyes while recalling those moments in his arms. With effort she kept her voice steady. "That was merely your overinflated ego at work, Mr. Marshall. Like so many men you imagine you can kiss a girl whenever the whim strikes you."

"Are you offering me a dare?" he asked softly. "Is it possible you'd like a repeat of yesterday's performance?"

Miriam MacGregor began writing under the tutelage of a renowned military historian, and produced articles and books—fiction and nonfiction—concerning New Zealand's pioneer days, as well as plays for a local drama club. In 1984 she received an award for her contribution to New Zealand's literary field. She now writes romance novels exclusively and derives great pleasure from offering readers escape from everyday life. She and her husband live on a sheep-and-cattle station near the small town of Waipawa.

Books by Miriam MacGregor

HARLEQUIN ROMANCE

2710—BOSS OF BRIGHTLANDS
2733—SPRING AT SEVENOAKS
2794—CALL OF THE MOUNTAIN
2823—WINTER AT WHITECLIFFS
2849—STAIRWAY TO DESTINY
2890—AUTUMN AT AUBREY'S
2931—RIDER OF THE HILLS
2996—LORD OF THE LODGE
3022—RIDDELL OF RIVERMOON
3060—MAN OF THE HOUSE
3083—CARVILLE'S CASTLE

MASTER OF MARSHLANDS

Miriam MacGregor

Harlequin Books

TORONTO • NEW YORK • LONDON
AMSTERDAM • PARIS • SYDNEY • HAMBURG
STOCKHOLM • ATHENS • TOKYO • MILAN

Original hardcover edition published in 1991
by Mills & Boon Limited

ISBN 0-373-03140-8

Harlequin Romance first edition August 1991

MASTER OF MARSHLANDS

CHAPTER ONE

THE sound of hoofs thudding softly on the new spring grass reached Lynn's ears. She turned slowly to face the man who cantered across the field towards her.

He reined the large chestnut gelding, dismounted and tethered it to the nearby boundary fence, then strode closer to stare at her with unconcealed interest. His dark grey eyes lingered momentarily on the blue jeans that clung to her slim hips, and on the green windcheater jacket that protected her from the sharp southerly breeze. They took in details of her flaming red hair, her clear complexion and the unflinching gaze of her green eyes.

'Are you looking for somebody?' he queried politely, his deep voice resonant.

The question startled her into wariness. 'I was hoping to see Stan,' she said, making it an excuse for her presence. Was this the owner of the neighbouring Marshlands property? she wondered.

Dark brows arched as his next words confirmed the fact. 'You're referring to Stan Bennett—my manager?'

She nodded, noticing the athletic form of his tall muscular figure.

He regarded her narrowly. 'Are you in the habit of meeting him here, near the boundary fence—or perhaps more privately, over there?' He nodded towards a clump of dark pines which sheltered a haybarn.

She allowed the hint of secrecy to pass over her head as she admitted coolly, 'It wouldn't be the first time I've spoken to Stan at the boundary fence.'

'Well—you can forget it for today because he's unlikely to loom over the horizon. He's taking an extended trip overseas. At the moment he's in Australia.' He paused then added thoughtfully, 'If you're in the habit of meeting him it's a wonder you didn't know that small fact. My cousin is not usually secretive.'

'I did not say I'm in the habit of meeting him,' she flashed, making an effort to hide her disappointment. Without Stan it would be more difficult to learn about his small son.

The man continued to regard her closely, his lids slightly narrowed. 'Have we met before?'

'I don't think so.'

'You look vaguely familiar to me. I feel sure I've seen that mass of red hair in some other place. It's like a flambeau.'

She laughed, brushing away the compliment. 'To me it's more like a dish of mashed carrots, especially when it's so unruly.' She raised a hand to smooth it against the wind.

'I prefer a flambeau. I almost saw sparks drop on the grass. And the smile you flashed just now—it also struck a familiar chord.' He looked at her expectantly. 'You're sure you've no recollection?'

'Of meeting you? None whatever.' How could she forget meeting a man with such charisma, or with a face as handsome as this one? His dark brown hair was well-groomed. His nose was straight, his mouth well-formed, the touch of sensuousness only adding to its appeal. His complexion was tanned, the tiny white lines at the corners of his eyes indicating squinting against the sun. He's an outdoor man, she thought, then said, 'I suppose you're Mr Marshall?'

'That's right. And you...? I presume you're from around these parts?' The dark brows arched again.

'No. I live in Wellington.'

'Ah—a city girl.' He ended on a long-drawn breath as his mouth twisted slightly.

She caught the note of disparagement in his voice. 'You're—allergic to city girls, Mr Marshall?'

'I avoid them as much as possible.' The words came coolly.

She felt nettled, but kept her voice casual. 'May I ask why?'

'They can be bad medicine—for country men.'

She looked at him without speaking, deciding that silence would be the wiser policy. It was possible he had the breakup between Stan and Delphine in mind, and at this early stage of her inquiry about their small son she had no wish to discuss them. What she learned about young Tony must come from her own observation, if this could be achieved.

His next words held a reprimand. 'I suppose—being a product of the big smoke and bright lights—you imagine you can climb fences and wander where you please in the wide open spaces, especially if there are mushrooms in the fields.'

'Thank you for hinting that I look thoroughly stupid. I happen to know that mushrooms appear in the autumn rather than in spring.'

'And being a city girl you probably couldn't care less about the fact that you're trespassing,' he pursued pointedly.

The accusation startled her. 'Trespassing? Yes—I suppose I am, but after all I've...' She bit off her words, stopping herself from saying she'd walked along this track towards the manager's house many times. It would reveal that she knew Delphine, and, while she saw no tangible reason for keeping the fact a secret, intuition warned her to hold the knowledge from this man—at least until she knew him a little better, although at the moment this seemed to be an unlikely prospect.

His eyes held curiosity as they regarded her closely. 'Yes? You were about to say that after all you've...what?'

She thought quickly then gave a slight shrug. 'Well—after all I've only come up the zigzag from Frog Hollow. Surely a neighbour, even a temporary one, is permitted to admire the view from your plateau without being accused of trespassing?'

She turned away from him to stare westwards where the small township of Waipawa sprawled from the river-bank towards higher ground. Beyond it farmlands stretched towards the long range of Ruahine mountains which lay at a distance of about twenty-five miles, their ridges now windswept and clear of winter snow, although their slopes were still streaked and patched with white depths that filled the gullies.

'You're staying with old Max Walker?' he asked.

'Maxwell Walker is my grandfather. I inherited this—this awful red hair from him.'

'Then I presume you're Miss Walker?'

'No. I'm Lynnette Nichols. My mother is his daughter. Most people call me Lynn,' she added, then wondered why she had offered this last snippet of information.

'My friends call me Blair,' he told her casually.

'How nice for them. Naturally, you mean the people who refrain from trespassing on your property.'

'Do you always prickle so easily?' Then, before she could snap a reply, he went on, 'How is old Max? I heard he'd been ill.'

'He had a bad chill which turned to pleurisy. The doctor put him in hospital, but he wasn't kept there for long. Mother and I thought he should have someone with him when he came home, so I decided to come to him for a period.' There was no need to expound upon her other reasons for wishing to visit her grandfather, she thought.

'That sounds as if you are out of a job, or have one that can be dropped at a moment's notice.'

'The latter, fortunately,' she said with a smile. 'My father is a doctor. I'm his receptionist, but we have a friend who stands in for me whenever necessary.'

'Your own private locum, in fact.'

'That's right. It means I can stay with Grandy for as long as I wish.' Or for as long as it takes to learn what I wish to know, she added silently to herself.

'Is Grandy your name for old Max?'

She nodded. 'Ever since I was a child.' She turned to look down at her grandfather's cottage. White-timbered and red-roofed, it stood on a rise beside an extensive swamp which lack of drainage had turned into a small lake inhabited by swans, ducks, swamp hens and frogs. The weed covering part of its surface lay like a green velvet blanket, while the clear water reflected the sky.

Blair's eyes followed her gaze. 'How long does he intend to live alone?' he asked.

She sighed. 'For as long as he has the health to do so, I suppose. My parents have tried to persuade him to live with us, but he just laughs at the idea.'

'Which is something you couldn't possibly understand,' he said, his tone decidedly mocking.

She felt irritated. 'Couldn't I? What makes you so sure about that assumption?'

'Naturally—because you're a city girl,' he snapped.

Anger made her flare at him. 'Mr Marshall, you do repeat yourself. Is it possible you've been hurt by someone who comes from a place larger than this small township of Waipawa?' Her voice rang with sarcasm.

'Definitely not—but I know someone who has,' he snapped abruptly, his jaw tightening.

He's thinking of Stan, hurt by Delphine, she decided, sensing the coldness that had crept into his manner.

'Then no doubt you understand all the circumstances behind that...that particular person's hurt?' The question came casually.

He hesitated momentarily before he said, 'I think so.'

'But you're not sure?'

'I'm sure enough to understand that women who have lived their lives in a city find difficulty in adjusting to country life. They miss the proximity of shops, theatre and every other activity to which they've become accustomed.'

'Unless they can find substitute interests in their new environment,' she pointed out. 'Wouldn't that make a difference?'

'Well—it might.' He reverted to the subject of her grandfather by saying, 'Old Max has reached the age of seventy and shouldn't be living alone. He'll probably tell you I've offered to buy his property. However, he refuses to part with it.'

'Are you saying you want him off Frog Hollow? Has he been trespassing?' she queried sweetly.

'Of course not,' he scoffed impatiently. 'Old Max can come and go as he wishes. His sheep are shorn or crutched in our woolshed. He enjoys pottering about during the shearing of our main flock and he gives a hand at docking time when the lambs lose their tails.'

'Then why do you want him to leave?'

He drew a deep breath as if still controlling his patience. 'Get this straight: I do not want him to leave. I merely wish to purchase Frog Hollow.'

Again her tone became sweet. 'Is this because you happen to be a trifle land-hungry? Shame on you, Mr Marshall.'

His jaw tightened as he gritted, 'You don't understand. It is simply that Frog Hollow was once part of Marshlands. It was sold by a previous owner of Marshlands who was in financial difficulties. That person later sold the remaining property to my great-grandfather.'

'And you would like to see Frog Hollow incorporated back into the main property?'

'Exactly. Besides, there's the lake. It's formed not only from seepage off the hills, but also from natural springs. It never dries up, therefore it's an excellent watering-hole during times of summer drought. And that's where Max could come in. He could live in the cottage as keeper of the lake. His job would be to see that animals did not become bogged. I'd pay him to do so.'

'You've suggested this to him?'

'Of course—but he still refuses to sell. He declares he has no intention of parting with his own roof over his head.'

Lynn laughed. 'I can just hear him. Grandy is very independent. He has always had his own roof, and I can't see him parting with it after all these years.'

'Not even for a good price?'

She shook her head. 'He doesn't need the money. Several years ago he owned a much larger property, but when Grandma died he could not bear to remain there without her. He sold and moved to another district, and that was when he bought Frog Hollow.'

'Let me assure you he wouldn't have had the opportunity if my father had been home at the time of its sale. Dad happened to be on an overseas trip—and believe me he was in a fine old rage when he knew he'd missed out on acquiring Frog Hollow.'

Lynn looked at him thoughtfully. Vaguely, she recalled this man's parents living in the Marshlands homestead when she had visited Delphine, who had been living in the manager's house. 'Your mother and father are still at Marshlands?' she asked casually, wondering if she would have to contend with them while learning about Tony.

'No; they've retired to live at Taupo, where Dad can fish all day and where Mother has become involved in charity work.'

'Then he'll no longer be mourning the loss of Frog Hollow.' She smiled. 'At least the place has kept Grandy nicely occupied for several years. He's maintained it well, so I'm sure you'll find it to be in good order when it is eventually gobbled up.'

'Gobbled up?' His mouth twisted into a line that betrayed anger. 'What the devil do you mean by that remark?'

'I mean when it loses its own identity and sinks into oblivion by becoming part of its neighbouring property.'

'Does that mean you might persuade Max to consider my plan?'

'Certainly not.'

'Yet you think the time will come?'

'I feel sure of it.'

'You happen to be psychic?' His tone held sarcasm.

'One doesn't need to be psychic to sense your determination, Mr Marshall. I suspect you to be a man who knows what he wants and who strides forward to grab it with both hands.'

'How would you know that, little lady?'

'Because what you *are* is written all over you. It drowns what you *say*.'

'I can believe the truth of that old maxim when I look at you.'

'What is that supposed to mean?' she demanded, her chin rising.

'I suspect you to be a typical burning bush: vibrant on the outside, but green, tender and loving below the surface.'

A flush rose to her cheeks but her expression remained serious as she said, 'That's something you'll never know, Mr Marshall.'

A soft laugh escaped him. 'Then we'll have to see about that.' He stepped closer, his dark grey eyes smouldering as an unexpected movement of his tanned fingers brushed her throat gently.

His touch caused her flesh to tingle and her flush to deepen. A small gasp escaped her as she moved away hastily, then she said with as much nonchalance as she could muster, 'It's time I went home to prepare Grandy's lunch.'

His eyes held amusement but all he said was, 'I suppose it's also time I went back to see how Gary is getting on.'

She was nonplussed. 'Gary? Who is Gary?'

'Gary Palmer. He's living in the manager's house and is working here while Stan is away. At the moment he's counting battens to be replaced in this boundary fence.'

'Oh. Well—goodbye.' She left him, and as she went towards the nearby zigzag she could almost feel his eyes piercing her back. She knew that he watched every movement of her walk, but she did not turn her head.

His voice called to her when she was halfway down. 'I'll see you around somewhere.'

She paused to look up at him. 'I doubt it. I intend to be kept rather busy.'

'Doing what?' he shouted as she continued to descend.

She stopped at the next sharp turn. 'Oh, this and that, and taking care of Grandy.' And other things, she added silently to herself.

The thought of Blair Marshall remained with her all the way back to the cottage. He's got a nerve, she decided, recalling some of the remarks he'd made. Burning bush, indeed! And the temerity of him to touch her throat upon such short acquaintance! Yet something about the recollection, plus the memory of the man's handsome face, left her feeling slightly breathless. But this, she told herself, was only because he was different from any of the men in her Wellington circle of friends.

When she reached the cottage the odours wafting from the kitchen indicated that lunch was already on the way with Grandy preparing one of his favourite meals. The elderly man stood before the electric stove gently stirring the sautéed onions that awaited the egg and milk mixture about to be poured over them. 'Sorry I'm late home, Grandy,' she said contritely.

Max Walker turned to look at her. His back was still straight in a slim figure of medium height, and, while his previously red hair was now grey, his blue eyes had lost nothing of their sharpness. 'You've been looking over some of your old haunts?' he asked.

'Yes. I couldn't resist climbing the zigzag,' she admitted.

'But no Delphine at the top.' His eyes glinted at her slightly flushed cheeks. 'Is it possible you met somebody else?'

She knew it was useless to brush Grandy's questions aside. 'Well, actually...I did meet a man...'

'Himself, was it?'

'Himself? Well, he said his name is Blair Marshall.'

'Ah, yes, to be sure. The master of Marshlands.'

'You make him sound like a tyrant.'

'He likes his own way.'

'Does that make him different from any other man?' she teased, then asked, 'How did you know I'd met someone?'

'By the smile playing about your lips—and there's a sparkle in your eyes,' he declared shrewdly.

She controlled the desire to ask more about Blair. Instead she said, 'That's only because I have so much to do. A challenge on my mind, you understand.'

'You mean because of the boy, or because of your stories? Learning about the boy will need patience, and redheads are seldom patient.'

'I'm aware of that fact.'

'As for your children's stories, I doubt that they're much problem. They seem to pop into your head, roll down your arms and slip off your fingertips to the typewriter.'

'I try to please them while teaching them something at the same time,' she admitted with shy modesty.

'At least you seem to please the publisher, and no doubt the Inland Revenue Department as well. As for young Tony Bennett, you'll have little difficulty in catching up with him. Frog Hollow is one of his favourite haunts.'

She looked at him eagerly. 'Are you saying he comes here to see you?'

'Certainly not. He comes to catch frogs.'

'Frogs! I suppose they're still here in their hundreds?'

'Of course they're still here. They've been here for years and are unlikely to leave a place that suits them so nicely. Didn't you hear their chorus of welcome when you arrived last evening?'

'I was too weary after the long drive from Wellington, but I heard them early this morning.'

'After a while you'll become so accustomed to their croaking you'll not hear them at all.'

'I'll never hear a croak without thinking of Frog Hollow,' Lynn said with a smile. 'Do you remember the time Delphine and I fell in the water? We were standing too near an edge that gave way.'

'I sure do. The yells from the pair of you brought me running.'

'And what did you do? You stood on the bank and laughed. You told us about the size of the eels living in the lake.'

Instead of sharing her amusement his mouth tightened.

She sensed his disapproval. 'I know you don't like Delphine, Grandy. I wish you'd try to understand.'

Frowning, he commented abruptly, 'Oh—I understand, all right. I understand that she should be home with her man and her young son. I've no time for desertion.' The last words were snapped.

'I suppose Tony misses her.' Lynn's voice held sadness.

'Of course the boy misses her. When you write you can tell her so.' His irritation bubbled.

'I'll not be writing until my observations give me something definite to report,' she told him, then veered away from the subject of Delphine by saying, 'I'm glad to see the black swans are still out on the lake.'

'Yes—they come and they go, although I think they look upon this place as home. I love those birds,' he admitted gruffly. 'They always remind me of the trip your grandmother and I took to Perth in Western Australia where there are so many black swans.' He fell silent, staring at the table while his mind looked into the past.

Lynn said gently, 'There are teal and grey duck out there too.'

But he was still with the swans. 'Did you know they mate for life? If one flies away it soon returns to find its mate. Not like one person I could mention,' he growled.

She ignored his reference to Delphine, saying, 'I noticed a blue heron out there. It's really a blueish grey and not at all like the lovely deep blue of the native swamp hens with their red legs and beaks. Don't you think they're pretty birds, Grandy?'

'The *pukeko*?' He gave the heavily built bird its Maori name. 'They've almost forgotten how to fly. Food and shelter is what brings them. Naturally, the boy thinks the lake is a fine place. It's full of tadpoles to be taken to school.'

Lynn laughed. 'In a jar of water, of course. He's probably the only boy in his class with a supply so close to home.'

'Well, he's been forbidden to come near the place— not that he takes much notice of that particular order. Stubborn, self-willed little imp—just like his mother.'

Lynn made an attempt to defend her friend. 'Be fair, Grandy. I dare say there's a sizeable splash of his father in him as well.'

'If there is, it's slipped out of sight,' the old man growled.

Lynn did not pursue the subject. Instead she veered away from it by asking, 'What are your plans for this afternoon, Grandy?'

Without hesitation he said, 'I'll have a short nap, then go to the club.'

'Would you like me to drive you there?'

He was shocked by the suggestion, his blue eyes glinting as he said, 'Good gracious, no. The day I can't drive my own car will be the day I must give up Frog Hollow. Fortunately, it hasn't come yet.'

His words startled her, causing her to look at him wordlessly. She hadn't thought of him reaching the stage of being unable to drive his car, but of course that time would come, as it did for most elderly people.

And when it did he'd be unable to go to the township for his food supplies, or to collect his mail from his post office box. And—horror of horrors—he'd be unable to reach his club where everything from the political situation to the latest cricket, rugby or soccer match was discussed and dissected.

In short, Grandy's days at Frog Hollow were now numbered, Lynn realised. His recent bout of illness had left him looking rather frail, causing his age to show more than usual. And the astute Mr Marshall who coveted the property would be well aware of this fact. He had only to sit and wait for it to come on the market.

Max's voice cut into her thoughts. 'This afternoon I'll keep away from the grumblers' table. It becomes a bore.'

'I presume that's where club members have a good moan?'

'That's it exactly. Old age makes some people grumble louder than the rest put together.'

She hesitated, then asked, 'What do you feel about old age, Grandy? Does it worry you?'

He shrugged. 'It's there and I can do nothing about it. It's the inevitable, so I count my blessings, especially at the moment.' His eyes twinkled as he looked at her.

'At the moment?'

'Of course. You're one of my blessings. I know that this cottage is about to be given the fright of its life with a good spring clean, and that all my socks are about to be darned.'

'I might not even raise a finger to do these things.'

'You will because you're like your grandmother when she was your age. When I look into your green eyes I see her all over again.'

Lynn's heart went out to him. 'Does that make you feel sad?'

'On the contrary, I'm delighted. I feel she's not so far away after all.'

It was mid-afternoon when Lynn stood on the small front veranda to watch her grandfather leave for his club. His red Ford was backed out of the double garage attached to the side of the cottage, then turned to be driven on to the country side-road which ran past the Frog Hollow stretch of water.

As he began to drive away a series of howls and barks rose on the air from the back of the house. Mick, his shaggy black and white Border Collie sheepdog, was registering loud protest at being left at home. The noise caused Max to put a foot on the brake, wind down the front passenger window and send out a whistle which resulted in an obedient silence.

For a few moments the car made a splash of bright colour against the green pastures, then it disappeared to twist and turn along the rises and falls of the undulating land. Lynn knew that half a mile along the road it would pass the entrance to the Marshlands homestead, and beyond that it would reach a main road where a turn would take it towards the Waipawa township.

She left the veranda and went through the french window which also served as the front door. Its small square panes of glass had already been cleaned, and she had transformed the living-room by the removal of dust and the newspapers left strewn in odd places. The open fireplace had been set in readiness for the evening's blaze and the hearth had been swept. A vase of purple lilac filled the air with a faint fragrance.

The cottage was old but comfortable. Originally built as accommodation for a shepherd, its kitchen had been modernised, although it still retained its old black coal range which gave warmth in the winter. The refrigerator had its deep-freeze compartment, and the washing-up sink was set in a stainless steel bench.

The two bedrooms opened off the living-room, the smaller being occupied by Max because it was conveniently closer to the bathroom and to the laundry with its toilet.

The front bedroom, occupied by Lynn, was larger because the end of the veranda had been closed off and added to it. The windows forming its alcove endowed the room with a sunny north-west corner which contained an extra divan bed and a table upon which rested her portable typewriter. Beside it were papers, carbons, correction fluid and a small pile of her published books, which were aimed at children of various ages.

After her arrival the previous evening Max had watched her set it all in order. 'The place is made for you,' he had said. 'An office and bedroom combined. I hope you'll occupy it for a nice long time. You know you're welcome to stay indefinitely.'

She had smiled. 'Thank you, Grandy.'

He had lifted a book from the table, its cover bright with farm animals. 'So this is what you do. I don't recall having such nice bedtime stories when I was a child. And these pictures are really beautiful.'

'They're done by an illustrator. I just do the stories,' she had explained.

He had sent her an anxious glance. 'Do you think you'll be able to work here? The place is very quiet. Inspiration might disappear.'

'Frog Hollow has an atmosphere of its own,' she had assured him. 'Ideas will come from observing all that goes on around the swamp or in the fields, especially at this time of the year when there are lambs.'

She had moved to the window to stare at a hillside where sheep with lambs at foot grazed the lush green pastures. Even as she had watched, a lamb had tried to drink at a ewe's udder but had been bunted away. It had then run to another ewe, but again had been given short shrift.

Lynn had felt shocked. 'Oh—did you see that?' she had exclaimed indignantly to Max who had joined her at the window.

'That lamb doesn't belong to either of those ewes,' he had explained. 'Each ewe knows its own lamb only too well—although there are some that desert their little one,' he had added drily.

She had remained silent for several moments, sensing the dig at her friend Delphine, but as she had no intention of discussing the subject so soon after her arrival she'd thought rapidly and said, 'I could do a story about a lamb that becomes separated from his mother and is bunted away every time he thinks he has found her. I'll call him Bobo. Do you like Bobo for a lamb's name?'

'Why not call him Tony? He's constantly searching for his mother.' His tone had still been dry.

Ignoring the remark, she had said, 'Bobo could get into all sorts of trouble during his search. I'll make it at shearing time when Mum comes out of the shed minus her wool and looking so different. It'll take him hours to find her. Grandy—I think I'll get a whole book out of Bobo.' She had become enthusiastic as the idea gripped her.

'You'd be wise to get yourself settled before that fertile brain takes control,' Max had advised. 'You haven't even finished hanging your clothes in the wardrobe.'

Lynn had laughed happily, glad to have latched on to a plot quite so soon after her arrival.

'Do you write only for small children?' Max had asked.

'No. Sometimes I concentrate on adventure stories for the older age-groups. They can become quite exciting.'

'Do you think you'll find adventure in these quiet hills?' The anxiety in his voice had indicated that he thought this would be difficult.

'It's possible.' She had gazed at the distant back country through half-closed lids, then had begun to speak as a vague idea swam into her head. 'The children in the big homestead are on holiday in the country. One night they see a light on the hills where there should be no light at that hour. Next day they go to investigate but can see nothing...'

Max had become intrigued. 'Yes, go on. There must be a reason.'

Lynn had shaken her head. 'One thing at a time. Bobo is waiting to leap on to the pages. And there are the birds on the lake. I must think of a story telling why the *pukeko's* legs and beak turned such a bright red, and why the swan's neck grew and grew, and about Freddie Frog who took singing lessons to enthral his lady love. You see—there's so much material here.'

Max had looked gratified. 'Good. It should keep you here for a nice long time, rather than for just a weekend.'

But now, as she left the veranda and wandered towards the wide shining stretch of water, the ideas for stories slid away from her, their place being taken by thoughts of the man she had met earlier that day. I'll see you around somewhere, he had said. When would that be? she wondered.

Memory of his attractive features and athletic virility caused questions to leap up and face her. Was there a woman in his life—a wife who lay in his arms each night? It was more than likely, but why should her thoughts move in such a direction?

Vaguely irritated with herself, she made an effort to drag her mind back to the material for children's stories, and as she felt Lucky, her grandfather's black cat, rub himself against her leg, she knew that he also must be featured. Tail aloft, he trod daintily, his instinct keeping him away from the treacherous edges that could fall away and drop into the water.

These animal stories, plus the ones concerning the inhabitants of the lake, would be of an educational nature, she decided. A frog he would a-wooing go? She knew that old rhyme to be incorrect because frogs did not a-wooing go. The males, she had discovered through research, sat in groups while blowing up their cheeks and croaking to attract the females to the trysting place. That was why Freddie Frog was taking singing lessons. The thought made her laugh.

And there was Mick the dog, now lying beside his kennel and waiting to take part in a story. His whimpers to be let loose came to her ears, but she dared not allow him off the chain without Grandy's presence to control his enthusiasm for rounding up every sheep in the district.

She sighed as her thoughts refused to be controlled, and, despite herself, they returned to Blair Marshall. Again she recalled the touch of his fingers against her throat—and again she told herself that some men had a colossal nerve.

But even while trying to whip herself into some form of righteous indignation, genuine anger would not register. Nevertheless she promised herself that she would stand well clear of him in future—that was if she ever saw him again.

Just as she made the decision, the still air was shattered by a sharp bark from Mick. She turned to see what had roused his interest, and then a movement against the green hill grabbed her attention.

On the higher land across the water she could see a man making his way down the zigzag. Nor was it difficult to recognise him as being the person she had met that morning. Himself, as Grandy would say. The master of Marshlands. Apparently she was to see him again sooner than she had expected.

CHAPTER TWO

LYNN remained motionless as Blair Marshall climbed the fence at the bottom of the zigzag. She watched him walk between the poplar trees growing along the lower slopes of the hill, and for one instant she was bitten by a crazy desire to run round the cottage end of the water, and along the far side of the lake to meet him. She then reminded herself that he had probably come to see Grandy, and to rush forward as though in glad greeting would only make her look foolish. He'd wonder about her eagerness—which was something she herself also questioned.

However, instead of pausing at the cottage in search of its owner he came towards her. 'Max is out,' he stated as though already aware of this fact.

'Yes. He's gone to his club. Did you wish to see him?'

'No. I knew he was away from home because I happened to be on our drive when his red Ford flashed past the entrance.'

'Oh.' Vaguely, she wondered why the sight of him made her breath quicken, then, as he merely continued to regard her in silence, taking in the flaming colour of her hair, she said, 'In that case, why have you come?'

'I felt a strong need to talk to you.'

'About what?' She looked at him wonderingly, her eyes vividly green as they reflected the surrounding pastures and the brightness of the weed on the lake.

'About Stan Bennett,' he admitted bluntly. 'Is it possible for you to tell me the truth?'

Her eyes blazed as a pink spot appeared in each cheek. 'Are you suggesting I'm a habitual liar?' she demanded indignantly.

'No—although there are plenty of people who skate round the truth, and no doubt it will depend upon what you decide to tell me.'

'And *that* will depend upon what you want to know.'

'OK, then perhaps you'll tell me why I get the feeling your acquaintance with Stan is more than casual?' His grey eyes held a piercing quality, almost as if defying her to deny his accusation.

She returned his gaze frankly. 'I've no idea. Perhaps you could tell me—and then we'll both know.'

'Possibly it's because you came looking for him. I'd like to know the true situation.'

'Situation?' She considered the word carefully. 'Why don't you come out into the open and tell me exactly what's on your mind?'

'Very well, I'll spell it out. The fact that you came looking for Stan this morning makes me wonder if it has been a habit for you to follow the track up there to a meeting-place.'

Her chin rose as her indignation began to grow, forming itself into a knot of anger that made her want to hit out at him. And then she guessed that his provocation was deliberate. Red-haired people were notoriously quick-tempered, and it was possible that he thought that if he goaded her sufficiently she'd burst forth with a few revealing indiscretions.

Watching her, he said abruptly, 'I have a niggling suspicion concerning your relationship with Stan—if you get my drift.'

'No, I do not get your drift, Mr Marshall,' she snapped crisply. 'I'd be grateful if you'd spit it out because I'm beginning to lose patience with this pointless conversation.'

'OK, then, here it is. Were you the reason for the breakup of Stan's marriage?' His mouth had tightened.

She stared at him, aghast that he should ask such a question, then she exploded furiously, 'So *that's* what you think! *How dare you?*'

'Well—*were you*?' His jaw seemed to thrust itself forward as he took a step towards her, gripped her arms and stared down into her face.

Her temper flared as she wrenched herself free. 'Considering it was I who introduced Delphine to Stan, I can't think of a more *idiotic* suggestion.'

His eyes narrowed. 'So, you know *her*?'

'Of course I know her. She was my neighbour in Wellington. At least, she lived in a boarding-house next door to my parents' home in the suburb of Kelburn. Please believe there was never anything between Stan and me.'

'OK. I believe you.' His voice held an echo of relief.

But she was not satisfied, and, drawing a deep breath, she enquired with forced sweetness, 'Are you forgetting I live in Wellington, Mr Marshall? Even you must realise it's a long way to come for a roll in the hay.'

'I said I believe you.' His voice had become harsh. 'It's just that I hated to think of your being the cause of their breakup.'

His words surprised her. 'Why would that be, Mr Marshall?'

But instead of answering her question he asked another. 'You communicate with Delphine?'

'Occasionally.' She saw no reason to deny this fact.

'So where is she now?'

'In London. Surely you're aware of her whereabouts? Doesn't Stan know where to get in touch with her?'

'I'm not positive. He's hardly spoken of her. In fact he's never even admitted the reason for the marriage breakup. That's why I felt suspicious when a girl as beautiful as yourself came searching for him in one of the back fields.'

She tossed the compliment aside. 'Do you always jump to conclusions in that presumptuous manner? Typical of a man, I must say.' Then she added with a hint of curiosity, 'Surely you'd have heard if Stan had been having an affair?'

He surveyed her coldly. 'You don't understand the situation. Until recently I've been away from Marshlands. It's called gaining experience on other properties. I didn't know what characteristics Stan might have developed, even if he is my cousin.'

'He was running Marshlands alone?'

'Of course not. My father was with him until he re-tired to live in Taupo where he spends all day on the lake, and when that happened Gary Palmer was em-ployed. It then became necessary for me to return to Marshlands, and by that time Delphine had left, and Stan had turned into a morose fellow who was definitely in need of a holiday.'

Lynn's normally smooth brow puckered as she said, 'I can understand Delphine being dissatisfied with her marriage—but I can't understand how she could have left her little boy.'

'Aren't you aware that she tried to take him with her?'

'No. I've heard very little of the affair, although I've wondered what made her leave Tony.'

His mouth twisted into a mirthless grin. 'The answer is simple. The court awarded custody of the child to his father.'

'I thought the custody of children was usually given to the mother.'

'Not when it deprives the child. It didn't take the court long to decide that life at Marshlands had more to offer the boy than a precarious existence with a solo mother. Besides, Stan was fortunate in having Maisie and Sandra to take over motherly duties.'

'Who are they?' She was unable to recall hearing the names.

'Maisie Bates is my housekeeper. Bert, her husband, attends to the garden and does odd jobs on the farm when we need an extra hand. They came to me when my parents took our previous housekeeper to live with them at Taupo.'

'And Sandra—who is she?'

'Sandra Walsh. Her parents live in the Waipawa township. She helps Maisie and is supposed to control young Tony, but I'm afraid she's finding him to be rather a handful.'

Lynn frowned. 'Why should he be a handful?'

'For the simple reason that he's a disobedient little lad who needs a firm hand. Despite anything Sandra says, he still suits himself. She becomes really mad with him.'

'Poor little Tony,' Lynn said softly, her heart going out to the boy. 'He's probably just like his father.'

He ignored the latter remark as he made a request. 'If he shows up round here you must send him home at once.'

'Is he likely to do that?' Lynn asked, remembering what her grandfather had said about Tony and the water.

'More than likely. He's going through the frog and tadpole stage. If he fell into the water he might not get out. He could sink into the muddy bottom and be held by weeds.'

The thought made her shudder as she again recalled the time the edge had given way beneath Delphine and herself. 'I can see how dangerous it could be for a small boy,' she admitted. 'Especially one who reaches out to catch tadpoles in a jar.'

'Good. At least we agree on that point.' He paused while his eyes examined every detail of her face, resting upon the fiery strands curling about the polo neck of her green jersey, then moving to watch the play of the dimple near the corner of her sweet and generous mouth.

'I'm glad you weren't the cause of that marriage breakup,' he said softly, his eyes holding an enigmatic expression.

'The day I break up a marriage will be the day,' she retorted. 'But why should you be concerned about any part I might have had in the affair?'

'Because I . . .' He fell silent, staring at her in a slightly puzzled manner, almost as if he himself wondered about this fact.

'Yes, go on,' she pursued. 'I'm interested.'

'If you must know, I'd hate to think you'd had a hand in it, but I'd still like to know why you went searching for Stan this morning.' He looked at her quizzically. 'Care to give me a reason?'

Her eyes flashed with impatience. 'For heaven's sake, I only wanted to ask him about Tony. Next time I write to Delphine I'd like to be able to tell her I've seen the boy and . . . and perhaps a little about him.'

His mouth took on a sardonic twist. 'What makes you think she'd be interested?'

Lynn became indignant. 'Of course she'd be interested. How can you doubt it?'

'Because she went away. She left the boy,' he pointed out bluntly. 'She'd been given access to see him, yet she takes herself all the way to London. What sort of a mother is that?'

Lynn found the question difficult to answer. They had wandered towards a seat built round the trunk of a massive weeping willow tree growing a short distance from the water, and as they sat beneath the hanging fronds she said, 'I feel sure she expects to have Tony with her—sooner or later.'

'Mere wishful thinking,' he snapped. 'With that custody order against her, she hasn't a chance.' Then he asked abruptly, 'Is it possible you can tell me what caused the marriage breakup?'

'Yes, I think so,' she said carefully.

'Then please enlighten me.'

'Actually there were two factors. Boredom was one of them.'

'Boredom?' He sounded shocked as he added, 'Boredom on a property so close to a town where there are numerous activities of interest to country women? There's the Countrywomen's Institute—there's an arts and crafts centre where they learn spinning, weaving, painting and pottery. Couldn't she have become involved in any of these things?'

Lynn sighed as understanding for Delphine's problems swept through her mind. 'Not one of those activities could compensate for the career she felt she'd thrown away.'

'Career?' he snorted. 'I wasn't aware that she'd sacrificed any sort of a career.'

Lynn regarded him with surprise. 'Surely you know what she was doing before she married Stan?'

He shrugged. 'You're forgetting that I wasn't around to learn these details. So what was this all-important career?'

'She worked with a Wellington publishing firm. Most of her time was spent assessing or editing manuscripts. You see, Delphine was an academic, rather than a spinner or potter or—or someone who did only housework.'

'Ah—*I told you so,*' he declared with triumph. 'Didn't I say that city girls are unable to adjust? So now we can understand why she became bored.' He paused thoughtfully, then said, 'You mentioned two factors. What was the other one?'

She hesitated then admitted, 'I'm afraid it was Stan himself. His attitude was of little help.'

'Stan? You're blaming him for their breakup? I don't understand.'

'It was really his possessiveness. Delphine was offered an office job in Waipawa, but Stan kicked up merry hell.

He would not allow her to take it, despite it being some-thing she needed.'

'Why not? Stan's a reasonable sort of fellow.'

'Not when it comes to somebody he imagines he owns body and soul. He expected her to be a chattel. He told her that as his wife she would toe the line. When he came indoors he expected her to be there, ready to submit to anything he—he had in mind.' The last words had brought colour to her cheeks, causing her to add hastily, 'In fact she felt she'd been turned into a mere servant.'

'Was there anything else?' His tone had become grim.

She considered the question then decided she might as well tell him all she knew, therefore her hesitation was only brief before she said, 'There was also the question of money. Before her marriage Delphine earned a very good salary, but of course it stopped when she left the firm.'

'That was to be expected.'

'After that she had to ask Stan for money, and he demanded that she accounted for every cent she spent. Stan was not accustomed to sharing his salary, you understand.'

He looked at her doubtfully. 'I find difficulty in be-lieving that Stan could be like this.'

'Then kindly learn a few facts before you launch into a full-scale criticism of Delphine.'

'Stan is not here for me to question him about these matters,' he pointed out with a touch of superiority.

'Nor would you do so if he were here,' she flashed at him. 'You'd dodge the issue by telling yourself it wasn't your concern.'

His eyes became hooded. 'What makes you so sure about that?'

'Because men always stick together. Even Grandy is against Delphine without knowing the facts.' She fell silent, watching two black swans gliding smoothly along the water, until at last she said, 'Well, at least I'll be able to tell her about Tony.'

'I shall tell you what to say about Tony.'

'No, thank you. I'd prefer to observe him for myself.'

'And I'd prefer you to leave well alone.' His words had become clipped, his brows drawn together.

Her eyes widened as she turned to him. 'What do you mean?'

'To put it bluntly, I want you to keep away from the boy.'

She became indignant. 'Surely you're joking?'

'Not at all. How long is it since you've seen him?'

'About eighteen months. It was just before...' The words died on her lips.

'Just before his mother left him to the mercy of other people,' he completed for her. 'It's possible Tony would remember you. In some way his young mind might connect you with his mother, and then, just as he's learning to do without her, his memory of her would be revived. And that, I consider, would be tragic.'

'You're trying to make him forget her?' Lynn demanded angrily.

'Don't you think it would be wiser?'

'No, I do not,' she said defiantly.

'You'd prefer to see the crying for her begin all over again?' His tone had taken on a bitterness.

She tried to defend her opinion. 'He was only four then. Now he has turned six and is probably accustomed to the situation.'

'Nevertheless, it's something I'll not risk, Miss Nichols—therefore I'll be grateful if you'll keep away from all areas of the Marshlands property.' His voice had become cold.

Her chin rose as she flared, 'I've no wish to set foot on as much as an inch of your precious domain, Mr Marshall.'

'And please don't encourage the lad to come here. In fact I'd like you to promise you'll make absolutely no attempt to see Tony. I hope I've made myself clear concerning this matter.'

Hot words rose to her lips but she bit them back while controlling her temper only with an effort. It would be unwise to quarrel openly with this man, she realised. It would only make her task more difficult, therefore she forced a smile as she said, 'Your wishes are very clear indeed. I shall not go chasing after him.'

'Good. I also hope I can trust you.' His voice had become hard.

The dimple beside her mouth came and went. 'You'll risk trusting a city girl, Mr Marshall?'

He ignored the taunt as he queried, 'I suppose your life in the city is one long round of gaiety?'

'Of course it is. Theatres, parties, and all that.' Her mind groped in vain for further entertainments.

His eyes held a hint of disapproval. 'It sounds an empty life. Have you no serious activities, apart from making appointments in your father's surgery, dusting the desk or straightening the magazines on the waiting-room table?'

'What would you mean by "serious activities", Mr Marshall?'

'I suppose I mean serious thoughts about your own future. Marriage, for instance. I can easily imagine a string of males beating a path to your doorway.'

A giggle caused the dimple to flash. 'Of course. Their sports cars are parked in a long line down the road while they fight on the front porch. Mother rushes out with a broom to sweep them away.'

'But no doubt she allows one to remain?'

'Naturally—the most eligible.'

'Ah, then you do have a boyfriend?'

'Is that any concern of yours?'

'Of course not.'

'Then why ask the question?'

'Why indeed?' Again his eyes examined her features, this time lingering on her lips before travelling lower to rest upon the area where her breasts caused two rounded mounds to rise beneath her green jersey.

The intensity of his scrutiny caused a flush to stain her cheeks. 'Your blatant stare is becoming very personal, Mr Marshall,' she informed him coldly. 'Am I the first city girl you've encountered?'

He remained serious. 'Let's just say you're one of the loveliest I've seen.'

His compliment caused the flush to deepen, and although she said nothing she became conscious of an inner satisfaction.

He went on, 'I'll also consider you to be one of the most sensible girls I've met—if you'll promise to make no attempt to see Tony.'

Lynn chuckled. 'I can't do that because I can see him now. Look—over there on the zigzag. Even from here I can see how much he has grown since I last saw him——'

Her words were interrupted by a shrill voice calling from across the water. 'Uncle Blair—Uncle Blair!'

An oath escaped Blair as he left her abruptly, his long strides carrying him purposefully round the cottage end of the lake and towards the track leading to the bottom of the zigzag. Lynn followed him gleefully, having to run to keep up with his pace, but when they reached the boundary fence he turned and faced her angrily. 'Stay there—just you keep off my property!' he snarled.

She forced a deliberate laugh. 'My goodness—what big teeth you have, Mr Marshall.' Then, looking at the boy on the other side of the wires, she said, 'Hello, Tony—remember me?'

Tony shook his head while staring at her doubtfully, then he looked up into the tall man's face. 'Mrs Bates

sent me to find you, Uncle Blair. She says to tell you a
stock agent has come to talk about buying cattle.'

'OK, let's go.' He grabbed Tony's hand and together
they went up the zigzag, the small boy racing to keep
beside him.

'I want to talk to that lady——' The young voice
floated on the late afternoon air, but there was no re-
leasing of the grip Blair held on his hand.

Lynn smiled to herself as she watched them ascend
the track, the boy's curiosity obvious as he sent glances
over his shoulder.

As soon as they had disappeared over the brow of the
hill she left the fence and returned to the cottage. In the
kitchen her thoughts remained with Blair Marshall as
she prepared the evening meal. But when she went into
her bedroom she paused to lift one of her books from
the alcove table, and this time her thoughts flew to
Delphine, who had been responsible for her small success
in the field of children's literature.

Returning to the living-room, she put a match to the
fire, and as she watched the leaping flames her mind
went back to the days when she had first known the slim,
dark-haired Delphine who was a few years older than
herself.

They had met in the cable-car which carried people
from the city centre up a steep grade to the suburb of
Kelburn. At the top, while walking along the footpath,
they had been surprised to learn that they lived next door
to each other, Delphine in a boarding-house filled with
office workers. She had confided that her job was with
a publishing firm, and, when Lynn had admitted to a
secret desire to write stories for children, Delphine had
laughed.

'You'll never do it by just thinking or talking about
it,' she said. 'You have to put pen to paper. Why not
make a start by writing one? I'll assess it for you. As it

happens I'm working in the children's books department.'

And so it began. Lynn, full of enthusiasm, wrote stories which were later typed in the office of her father's surgery whenever the opportunity arose. They were then given to Delphine for criticism, but, despite the thought and labour put into them, they were pulled to pieces with ruthless honesty.

'Try again,' Delphine ordered. 'You're getting there.'

But Lynn felt she was getting nowhere. Nevertheless the tenacious streak in her nature forced her to try again—and again—until she almost reached the stage of giving up. And then the day came when the help she had received from Delphine bore fruit. It took the form of a long envelope which arrived in the mail.

Scarcely able to believe her eyes, she saw it was from the firm for which Delphine worked. Her fingers shook as she tore it open, and then her eyes almost blurred as she read that they thanked her for submitting her manuscript, *The Little Grey Donkey*, which they would be pleased to accept. Publication would take place during the following year for the six- to ten-year age-group. An agreement was being prepared.

Lynn read the letter several times, her excitement growing more intense with each unfolding of the single sheet of paper topped by its letterhead. Next year she would actually have something in print—her dream of being a children's author would be realised, and she had Delphine to thank for the miracle.

Later, when the bubbling excitement had simmered down sufficiently to allow clear thinking, she read the first line again. 'Thank you for submitting your manuscript.' But she had *not* submitted a manuscript. She had merely handed Delphine several stories concerning the adventures of Donald Donkey who, having discovered an open gate, had trotted out into the wide world beyond the confines of his paddock.

'Not very original,' Delphine had commented, flicking rapidly through the pages.

Lynn had sighed. 'Well—if you'll just give me a criticism. After that I'd better give up.'

'Don't you dare,' Delphine had rasped at her.

And now it seemed that the stories had been combined to form a book. And it was Delphine who had placed it under the nose of the person who would accept it for publication. It was Delphine who had groomed her efforts towards this moment.

At a later date Lynn met the publisher, who expressed surprise to discover that she was only seventeen. He encouraged her to continue with her writing, and even admitted he liked the style she was developing. She then knew she must have her own typewriter—a portable she could put in the car when visiting her grandfather at Frog Hollow.

But now, while looking back to those past days, Lynn realised it had been a mistake to tell Delphine about Frog Hollow.

Delphine's hazel eyes had been filled with envy as a sigh of dejection had escaped her. 'You have a place to visit in the *country*?' she almost moaned. 'You're so *lucky*. How I'd love a weekend away from the noise, the hustle and bustle of the city—to say nothing of having a few days away from that boarding-house.'

Her words resulted in a visit to Frog Hollow, the journey in Lynn's small car taking a little less than four hours. It was something she could do for Delphine, she thought, and heaven knew she was deeply in debt for all the help she had received.

But how was she to know that Delphine would meet Stan Bennett, who happened to call on Grandy with a request for assistance in tailing the lambs? And how could she possibly know they would fall for each other like a couple of shooting stars dropping from the night sky? How was she to know they'd begin by twinkling at each other, and that soon they'd be sparkling with impatience to get married?

The wedding was a simple register office ceremony which took only a few minutes to perform. In fact the speed of it left Lynn wondering if they were really married. She was their only bridesmaid, and she still felt dazed when the few friends who attended gathered in a restaurant for a wedding lunch, and where photos were taken.

But it was all too rapid. Stan and Delphine did not know each other well enough, and the marriage lacked the understanding that would have given it stability. Despite the birth of Tony it did not last.

It was not surprising that incompatibility had raised its head, Lynn thought as she recalled how the loss of a career had begun to niggle at Delphine. Nor was this helped by Stan's possessiveness towards the money he brought into the house.

Further reminiscences took her back to one of her weekend visits to Frog Hollow. She had climbed the zigzag and walked across the field path to visit Delphine, but even before she had reached the door of the manager's house she heard the raised voices.

Stan was in a rage. He'd been trapped into marriage, he shouted.

Delphine screamed that he could be free any moment he liked. She would leave. She would go home to her mother in London and take Tony with her.

Stan roared dire threats about what he would do if she dared to remove *his* son.

At that moment Lynn raised her hand and knocked on the door, hoping her presence would stop the quarrel. Stan then stormed out of the house while Delphine wept that she couldn't take any more of this traumatic existence with him. Nor was it long before Lynn heard that Delphine had actually left him.

But despite Grandy's disapproval of Delphine, and Blair Marshall's obvious siding with Stan, Lynn's sympathies were with her friend. And again she remembered that her own books for children had seen publication only through Delphine—therefore the report she'd been asked to make on Tony took the proportion of a most sacred trust. It was something she *must* do, but the burning question was how to make a beginning.

The answer came next day, which was much sooner than Lynn could have hoped for. And it happened in a way which surprised her because, although she expected to go searching for Tony, the boy simplified matters by coming to her.

It happened during the afternoon when she carried a pen and scribbling-pad to the willow tree seat. Nearby the thick clumps of hawthorn, now past their massed pink and white flowering, sheltered her from the westerly breeze which blew the green weed to the other side of the lake. But even as she began to wonder what lay beneath its blanket-like surface a sound floated on the air.

A glance at her watch told her it was the school bus, a vehicle which collected children from the school gate, then travelled along country roads to drop them at various places. There was no reason for it to stop at Frog Hollow, therefore she was surprised to hear its brief pause at their entrance.

Moments later she saw Tony, small schoolbag slung over his shoulder, walk towards the cottage. He stepped on to the veranda and peered into the room, his nose pressed against one of the square panes of the french window. Then, on discovering the room to be empty, he left the veranda and made his way towards the water.

Lynn sat motionless, waiting for him to become aware of her presence beneath the hanging fronds of the willow tree. It took only an instant for him to do so, and then he ran towards her. There was a long silence while he examined her carefully, and when he spoke his voice betrayed disappointment. 'You're not my mother.'

Her heart went out to him. 'No. I'm Lynn. Do you remember Lynn?'

He shook his head.

'You saw me yesterday. Did you think I might be your mother, and so you came back to have another look at me?'

He nodded.

'Does Uncle Blair know you've come here?'

Again he shook his head.

She looked at him thoughtfully, feeling delighted by this unexpected encounter, and realising she must make the most of it. He was a slimly built boy who would one day be tall, she noted. His dark hair fell in a fringe across his brow, and he looked at her with hazel eyes which gave him a resemblance to Delphine. But not to be denied, and even more pronounced, was the definite likeness to his tall brown-haired father.

A question leapt into her mind. 'Why didn't the bus stop at the Marshlands entrance?'

'Because I didn't pull the cord, so it went past. The other kids yelled at the driver but he took no notice till we got here—then he stopped the bus and told me to run home or he'd put a mighty big flea in my ear.'

'Doesn't anyone meet you at the drive entrance?'

'Sandra was there. She shouted at the driver but he didn't hear. She jumped up and down—I reckon she got mad as mad.'

Lynn hid a smile. 'Why didn't you pull the cord?'

'Because I wanted to come here.' The statement came frankly.

'So you didn't just forget—and it wasn't that you were unable to reach the cord. This is really a planned visit.'

He nodded without speaking, admission shining from his eyes.

She tried to remain serious but the effort was too much. A laugh escaped her as she said, 'What shall I do with you?'

A smile broke over his face as he looked at her hopefully. 'Have you got anything to eat? When I come home from school Mrs Bates gives me cookies. She says growing boys gotta be fed.'

Lynn laughed again. 'Very well—we'll see what we can find.' She stood up, left her pad and pen on the seat, then led him to the kitchen where she poured milk into a glass and spread wholemeal scones with butter and raspberry jam.

Watching her, he said, 'Mrs Bates makes me wash my hands.'

'Top marks for her,' Lynn applauded, then guided him to the bathroom where she put warm water in the washbasin. 'Use plenty of soap,' she advised as the water turned grey.

A few minutes later he sat at the kitchen table and ate with relish while Lynn watched the scones disappear. Here was the opportunity to learn a little about his days, she realised—but where to begin? Tentatively she put out a feeler. 'I suppose Mrs Bates gets you ready for school?'

'No. Sandra makes me wash my face and put on my school clothes. She cuts my school lunch while Mrs Bates makes me eat my porridge. After that Sandra makes me clean my teeth before we go.'

'To catch the school bus?'

'No. I only come home on the bus. In the morning she takes me in a red car that my mummy used to drive.'

Lynn recalled the small red Fiat that had been put at Delphine's disposal, but she then shied away from further mention of his mother by asking, 'Do you like riding on the school bus?'

'Not much. I gotta get on it straight after school. I can't stop for a while and play with any of the other boys.' His tone had become full of complaint but brightened as he added, 'Dad says I can have a bike when I'm a big boy.'

'You've a few years to wait before that happy day arrives,' Lynn pointed out, realising that his main problem was loneliness. Apart from breaks between lessons and lunch hour at school, he lacked the playtime company of other children. Then, visualising him sitting at a desk in the classroom, she asked, 'Which lessons do you like best?'

'I don't like *maths*,' he declared almost fiercely. 'The best time is when teacher reads a story to us.'

'Some day you'll read stories for yourself,' she told him.

'I can now, a bit . . .'

'Then we'll hear how well you can recognise words.' She went to her bedroom where she selected two of her books which were near his age-group, and bright with illustrations of farm animals.

The words in the first book she placed before him were recognised with ease, but with the second and more difficult book he became hesitant. 'What's this word, Lynn?' he asked.

Before she could reply a shadow appeared at the open doorway as Blair Marshall's cool voice said, 'Perhaps it's *obedience*—a word you've not yet learnt, my young friend.'

The boy grinned happily. 'Hello, Uncle Blair—we're having scones and jam.'

Blair scowled. 'Yes, I can see we're being fed and entertained as well.' He turned to Lynn, his jaw thrust forward, his eyes cold with anger. 'What did you do? Did you bribe the bus driver to bring him along the road and drop him off at Frog Hollow?'

CHAPTER THREE

LYNN returned Blair's accusing glare unflinchingly. 'Are you actually accusing me of bribing the bus driver? I mean, is that what you really believe?'

His mouth became a thin line. 'It's difficult to know what to believe—especially when it involves certain people.'

'Which means you consider me to be a liar.' A laugh escaped her. 'Poor Mr Marshall, he's so confused! Perhaps he should grab the bus driver by the scruff of the neck, give him a good shaking and then explain what it's all about.' The thought made her giggle.

'Very funny,' he gritted.

'Or you could ask Tony how he happens to be here. I dare say he'll tell you the truth, even if I can't be relied upon to do so.'

Blair looked at the boy. 'At the moment he's incapable of telling anything. His mouth is positively *stuffed*.'

Tony chewed rapidly, swallowed, then appealed to Lynn. 'Have you gotta scone for Uncle Blair? Uncle Blair needs a scone with lots and lots of jam.'

'He sure does!' Lynn laughed as she turned to the man who still remained at the door. 'Won't you come in and sit down? The kettle is boiling, so I'll give you a cup of tea as well.'

'No, thank you.' His clipped tone emphasised his refusal as he entered the room and stood frowning at the boy.

Lynn went on calmly, 'Oh, well, I shall make tea just the same.' And while she did so she listened to Blair speaking to the boy.

'Why didn't the school bus stop for you?' he demanded. 'Didn't you pull the cord?'

'No.' The word was accompanied by a vigorous shake of the head.

'Why not?' Blair's voice had become stern.

'Because I wanted to come here. I wanted to see Lynn.'

'And she welcomed you with open arms. Haven't you been told you must not come to this place? It's dangerous for little boys.'

'And for big boys,' Lynn flashed unguardedly, then could have bitten her tongue. Fool—what would he make of that stupid statement? But perhaps it had slipped his notice.

It had not. Slowly he turned to face her, his eyes boring into her own. 'Big boys, Miss Nichols? What is that remark supposed to—er—indicate?'

'Nothing—nothing at all,' she assured him hastily.

'Is it possible that big boys could also be welcomed with open arms?'

'Certainly not,' she snapped, still irritated by her own lack of discretion, and by the added pinkness in her cheeks.

'That's a pity,' he replied mildly. 'It could be a way of leading to a closer understanding of the situation.'

'You mean by cajoling *me* towards *your* way of thinking?'

'Not at all. You might even convince me——'

Her laugh cut into his words. '"Convince a man against his will—he's of the same opinion still,"' she quoted.

'Oh, well, it was just a suggestion.' He turned again to Tony. 'You'd better know that Sandra is very upset. In fact she's hopping mad with you. She waited at the end of the drive but the bus just rolled past. She said you grinned at her through the window—that you even had the temerity to send her a wave.'

Tony's eyes widened. 'What's tem...tem...what you said mean?'

'It's another word for audacity—or effrontery.'

Lynn spoke in a dry tone. 'I'm afraid those words are over his head, Mr Marshall. You're expecting too much of a boy who is only six. I happen to know about words for children...' She stopped abruptly, casually removing the books from the table and feeling thankful that they were lying face downward.

Tony said, 'Please, may I have another scone?' The hazel eyes were pleading as they gazed at Lynn.

'Yes, of course.' She split, buttered and spread it with jam, placed the two halves together and handed it to him.

Blair spoke to the boy in a more kindly manner. 'You will eat it on the way home, old chap. You will go round the end of the lake, up the zigzag and across the field track. You will go to Sandra and explain why you didn't get off the bus—and you will say you are very sorry for causing her to be so upset. Is it understood?'

Tony nodded wordlessly.

Lynn had expected Blair to leave with the boy, but this, she soon realised, was not his intention. Instead he stood in the doorway while watching Tony's progress round the end of the water, and then instinct warned that his wrath was about to descend upon her own head.

Hastily, she poured two cups of tea. 'Sit down, Mr Marshall,' she invited affably. 'I know you're just bursting to blast my head off—so you might as well do it in comfort. Is that tea strong enough? Do you take milk and sugar?'

He regarded her with an amused glint in his grey eyes. 'Are you always quite so incorrigible, Miss Nichols? Or is this merely an attempt to take the wind out of my sails?'

She looked at him wonderingly. 'What can you possibly mean, Mr Marshall? Really—I don't understand.'

'Are you trying to leave me flapping helplessly by making a deliberate attempt to soothe my anger with a display of hospitality? You must think I'm an utter half-wit if you imagine I can't see through your little tactics.'

She forced sympathy into her voice. 'Are you not accustomed to being offered hospitality, Mr Marshall? Is this because you always appear to be so cross?'

'I am not cross,' he snapped irritably.

'No? You could have fooled me. It's the only way I've seen you.'

'I said, *I am not cross*.'

'Then prove it by drinking your tea.'

'It's just that I'm concerned about the boy.'

'You're worrying needlessly, so let's chat about something else. You're allowed to talk with your mouth full of scone and raspberry jam.' She pushed the plate towards him.'

'I must say they're delicious.'

'That's because they're freshly baked. When I'm here I make them each day because Grandy likes them.'

He looked about him. 'Didn't I see children's books? Are they also here for Grandy? I didn't think Max had quite reached his second childhood in the matter of reading material.'

'Oh, they just happened to be here,' she explained evasively, while acknowledging to herself that she was not yet ready to divulge her activities in this particular field. No doubt he would learn of it at a later date, but at present her instinct warned that now was not a suitable time. He would be certain to look upon it as a further enticement for the boy to visit her.

Pondering these thoughts, she was unaware that a shaft of late afternoon sunshine was now slanting through the kitchen window, catching her mass of unruly hair in a noose of flame. The same shaft caressed the twin rise of breasts beneath her bright green woollen jersey, causing a reflection that turned her eyes to emeralds.

And when she became aware that he was regarding her closely, her gaze became direct as she said, 'Something about me continues to worry you, Mr Marshall?'

He watched the play of the dimple beside the sweet fullness of her mouth then said quietly, 'I'll say it does. I consider you to be positively dangerous.'

The words startled her, causing her to straighten her back as she demanded indignantly, 'What on earth are you talking about?'

'Surely you can work that out for yourself?' he commented with a wry twist to his mouth.

'No, I can't. I've no idea what you are trying to say. The fact that you're antagonistic towards me sticks out a mile—but why I should be considered *dangerous* is beyond my comprehension.' Glaring at him she paused for breath before adding, 'Perhaps you'd be good enough to explain yourself.'

'I would if I could,' he informed her soberly. 'At the moment it can only be described as an instinctive fear that warns me against a hidden snare.'

Her eyes widened with incredulity. 'A *snare*? Do you mean a trap of some sort?'

'Something like that,' he admitted, his tone grim.

'And this ... hidden snare ... involves me?'

He hesitated then said, 'It's more likely to involve results. I mean results from the fact that you are here.'

'But you know why I'm here. Is it necessary to remind you that Grandy needs someone to care for him—at least for a while?'

'Personally I consider he needs someone older than yourself, and on a more permanent basis.' He regarded her thoughtfully before asking in a casual tone, 'How long did you say you'll be with him?'

'I didn't say. But why should it worry you?'

He looked at her without speaking, his penetrating gaze giving the impression that he sought to read her inmost thoughts, and then he asked softly, 'What have you got in mind?'

'I can sense the underlying fear in that question, Mr Marshall. Tell me, are you always so apprehensive about strangers who dare to stray near your boundary line, or who climb the zigzag to look at the view?' Her last words were flung at him scathingly.

'Only when I'm forced to wonder about their plans.'

'You couldn't possibly imagine I have any plans concerning yourself,' she said, then longed to recall the suggestion.

The smirk that played about his mouth caused his expression to become mocking. 'Any plans concerning myself would be a waste of time,' he informed her in a sardonic tone. 'I have myself well under control where women are concerned.'

She stared at him with wide-eyed interest. '*Really?* Are you saying you dislike women?'

'I'm saying I have little to do with them. I'm far too busy.'

She continued to regard him with the interest she would give to a rare specimen. 'I must say you surprise me. Most men find at least a little time for women.'

He frowned. 'What do you mean? Why should it surprise you to learn that I'm not entangled with a female?'

She left the table abruptly and carried the empty cups to the bench where she turned to stare at him. 'Not for one moment would I have believed you were like *that*. And you're not even wearing an earring of any sort!'

His face darkened as he exploded, 'What the hell are you going on about?'

'Well, if by your own admission you're so very allergic to women, I can only presume you belong to the...the gay fraternity. I'm told they wouldn't even want to kiss a girl...' The words were regretted the moment they left her lips, and, acutely embarrassed at having broached such a subject, she turned her back to him, then bit her lip as she stood gazing through the window set above the sink.

But he was on his feet in an instant, an oath escaping as he swung her round to face him. 'I'll soon put you right on that score,' he gritted fiercely, then pinned her arms to her sides while pressing her against his body.

The unexpectedness of it caused her to catch her breath, and although she struggled to turn her face away his mouth descended upon her own in a kiss that betrayed domineering ferocity rather than affection of any sort.

She knew that his breathing had quickened, and that her own pulses were beginning to race. Nevertheless she wrenched her mouth free. 'You...you've got a nerve,' she spat furiously, her eyes glittering, her cheeks turning scarlet.

His face became expressionless. 'I felt sure you wanted to know whether or not I can kiss a girl.'

'I did not—I couldn't care less!' she exclaimed.

'Yet I feel you sound doubtful. Let me show you again.'

'Certainly not—there's no need.'

But despite her protest he proceeded to do so, although this time the kiss was less fierce as he teased and nuzzled her lips seductively before claiming them with a depth that betrayed an inner passion that pleaded to be set free.

Her senses were reeling when his mouth left her own, and as his arms released her body she could only blink at him in a dazed manner. 'You—you had no right to take such a liberty,' she declared, making an unsuccessful attempt to sound really angry.

'You yourself made it necessary,' he informed her coolly. 'Your outrageous suspicion that my preference did not lie in the direction of the fair sex gave me the right to prove I am well able to kiss a girl as she deserves to be kissed. Are you now convinced about that important fact?'

She had a strong desire to giggle, but decided to nod without speaking.

'I'm also capable of much more,' he murmured, his eyes hooded.

'I'm sure you are,' she admitted faintly while trying to control the tremor in her voice. 'But now...I...I think you should leave.'

'Why?' His hands went to her shoulders as he looked down into her face. 'Are you afraid of being kissed again? Is it because you fear you'll find yourself craving for more—and more—of the same?'

The audacity of the suggestion made her snap furiously. 'You flatter yourself, Mr Marshall. Just watch your step—or you'll find yourself falling under the snare of my own particular wiles.'

'I can cope with your wiles—you little firebrand,' he murmured, his voice strangely husky.

As the words ended the grip on her shoulders tightened, and again he snatched her to him. His lips claimed her own once more, but this time the kiss was gentle. It was seductively caressing as it teased her senses while causing her heart to throb, and while removing all desire to struggle against him.

At last it ended, but without removing his arms he continued to look down into her face. 'That was better,' he commented in a satisfied tone. 'You almost responded. Now—will you promise?'

She was puzzled. 'Promise what?'

'To remember my request concerning Tony. If he turns up at Frog Hollow—just send him home.'

'I can see that he must not be allowed to start fretting again,' she said without making any sort of promise.

'Then at least we're getting somewhere,' he applauded, again speaking with satisfaction.

A smile of understanding broke over her face, and, gazing up at him, she exclaimed, 'So that's what those kisses were all about.'

Frowning, he became wary. 'What are you trying to say?'

'Well, naturally, they were merely a means of persuading me to your way of thinking. They were, in fact, a sample of your own particular—wiles. Isn't that so, Mr Marshall?'

His voice hardened as he snapped, 'Your memory must be short if you've forgotten what really caused them. Something to do with my own preferences, if I recall correctly. However, if they've helped to guide you towards my way of thinking, then perhaps another kiss wouldn't go amiss——'

She was torn between raising her face and telling him to go home when the sound of a bark filtered into the kitchen. It caused Lynn to say, 'That was Mick. Grandy must be back from going round his flock. He's been watching for late lambs.'

Max entered the kitchen a few minutes later. He greeted Blair affably, but as he sank into a small easy chair beside the wood range he was unable to disguise his weariness. Then, as his eyes took in the sight of the teapot, he said, 'That's just what I need.'

'I'll make a fresh pot,' Lynn said, at the same time feeling thankful that there were two scones left.

Blair spoke to Max. 'I notice you're still breeding black sheep.'

The older man sighed. 'Yes. I never thought I'd see the day when I'd have an entire flock of them, even if it's only a small mob. I seem to have become a supplier of natural dark wool for people who belong to the numerous spinning and weaving groups in the district. They come to examine the length of staple, the texture of the fibre and the various shades ranging from light to dark greys.'

Shearing arrangements were then discussed, and as she listened to the conversation Lynn learned that next month a gang of Maori shearers would arrive at the Marshlands woolshed. The flock of three thousand Romney sheep would be shorn, and when that task had been completed the small mob from Frog Hollow would lose their wool. It was imperative, she knew, to keep the black wool from becoming mixed with the white wool.

Blair said, 'Maisie Bates has caught the spinning bug. She's waiting for your lot to be shorn.'

'Is that so? Then she can come to the woolshed while they're being done. It'll give her first choice.' Max took a scone from the plate Lynn had placed beside him.

Blair said apologetically, 'I'm afraid you've been eaten out of house and home. I've done my best, while Tony did more than his share.'

Max became interested. 'The boy was here? You brought him here?'

'Definitely not. I found him here and sent him home.' He then changed the subject by adding, 'I must compliment you on your cook.'

'She's just the best.' Max grinned, sending a fond glance in Lynn's direction. 'No doubt she's told you of her plans and activities?'

'No, she has not,' Lynn cut in sharply while feeling a sudden irritation towards her grandfather. 'Nor has she any intention of doing so.'

Blair looked at her with interest, his brows raised. 'Plans? Activities? What could they be?' he drawled, making no effort to disguise his curiosity.

But Lynn was not in the habit of expounding on her books for children, therefore she said firmly, 'They are my own concern entirely, Mr Marshall—and I'll thank Grandy for remembering that fact.'

'Sorry I spoke,' Max said with a trace of huffiness. 'And what's this Mr Marshall business? Can't you call him Blair?'

Blair laughed. 'It's Lynn's way of keeping herself out of reach.' He stood up to leave, turning to Lynn as he did so. 'I trust you'll not forget?' he said in a voice that had a significant ring to it.

'Forget?' Startled, she looked at him blankly. Was he referring to their recent embrace? The thought made her colour rise.

The reminder came quietly. 'My request concerning Tony—if you care to remember.'

'Oh, *that*.' Her voice sounded hollow.

'Yes, *that*. Did you imagine I could mean anything else?'

It was impossible to miss the mocking glint in his eyes, therefore she responded with studied coolness, 'What else could there be?'

'Indeed, what else?' He then nodded briefly to Max, and moments later he was striding round the top end of the lake towards the fence, which he vaulted with ease.

Lynn stood at the back door watching his progress up the zigzag. He's annoyed with me, she thought. He's got the pip because I didn't explain about plans and activities. And then a feeling of unreality gripped her as she recalled that only a short time earlier she had been in his arms and that he had kissed her.

The memory brought a feeling of warmth, and, although she made an effort to whip herself into a state of righteous indignation, genuine anger failed to register. And then honesty forced her to admit that the feel of his arms about her body had been rather nice—and that the pressure of his lips on her own was certainly something to remember.

Max spoke from behind her. 'What was all that talk about forgetting? I failed to get the hang of it.'

She turned to find his blue eyes regarding her intently. 'Oh, he wanted me to make a promise, but I did not make it.' She went on to tell him how Tony's failure to get off the school bus had brought Blair Marshall

stamping to their back door. And as she finished by
telling him of Blair's disapproval, she became aware that
her grandfather was regarding her seriously.

'He's right, of course,' Max commented. 'You must
not encourage the youngster to come here. There's also
the matter of discipline. The boy must learn to do as
he's told.'

'But Grandy, how can I send him away? I have a strong
urge to give him love, to cuddle him in my arms——'

Max snorted. 'You'd be much wiser to find a bigger
boy to cuddle; a man to hold *you* in *his* arms.'

'Don't be silly, Grandy.' Lynn giggled but found herself
unable to look at the old man.

'Now this fellow Blair Marshall—I believe he's
unattached.'

'Is that a fact? So what, Grandy?'

'He's got stability,' Max went on. 'He's a thoroughly
sound individual with his feet on the ground.'

'Where else would they be, Grandy? Up in the air?'
Lynn spoke flippantly while beginning to feel slightly
hysterical.

'You know what I mean,' he growled. 'And let me tell
you this—he's most eligible. His bride will be carried
into a lovely home surrounded by a thousand acres of
first-class undulating country.'

'How nice for her. Does that include Frog Hollow? I
suppose you know he covets this place?'

'Of course I know—and it's understandable considering it was once part of Marshlands.' He paused thoughtfully then added, 'Well, he'll get it only if he marries
you.'

Shock caused Lynn's jaw to sag. 'Wh-what are you
saying?'

'You're in line to inherit it. I might drop a hint in his
ear.'

She laughed, refusing to take him seriously. 'You do
that, Grandy, and when he's on his knees begging for

my hand I'll tell him it's only because he knows I'm Queen of the Frogs.'

Max remained unsmiling. 'I mean it, lass. When I shove off, this place will be yours.'

The thought of his death horrified her. 'Please don't talk about dying, Grandy...I-I can't bear it.'

'Nevertheless, we all have to go, and my day will turn up sooner or later. When it does I want to know that Mick will be cared for. I don't want him to be sold to a stranger who might put a boot into his ribs because he doesn't understand what's wanted of him.' He paused, looking at her seriously as he added, 'Promise me—if I pop off suddenly you'll turn to Blair at once.'

'Turn to Blair...?'

He went on, turning away from her surprised eyes, 'Mick knows him, and I'm sure he'd give the dog a good home. And I reckon Maisie Bates would see to Lucky's welfare,' he concluded with a heavy sigh.

It was the sigh that roused her suspicions, and then enlightenment dawned as his intentions struck her with force. 'Grandy—you cunning old fox, you're *pushing* me at Blair. Well, it won't work.'

'What won't work?' he demanded, still without looking at her.

'Your anything but subtle effort at matchmaking.'

'I feel sure I saw a gleam of interest when he looked at you.'

She laughed. 'Pure imagination. I've often wondered who endowed me with my own, and now I know. Dear Grandy, you'd better understand that I'm not one of his favourite people.'

'Because of the boy? You'd be unwise to allow that child to come between you.'

'You're away ahead of yourself, Grandy. There's nothing for him to come between. For Pete's sake, I've only just met Blair Marshall.'

'Things can happen quickly,' Max pointed out sagely. 'Personally I consider you'd be wise to obey Blair's wishes by sending Tony home.'

She shook her head as her decision rooted itself firmly in her mind. 'No, Grandy,' she said quietly. 'If he comes again I shall not turn him away. That little boy can do with all the love he can find, and if he does begin to associate me with his mother—as Blair fears—it might make him feel she's not so far away after all.'

Max eyed her sternly. 'Can't you see that your philanthropic ideas will cause trouble between neighbours?'

'What big words you use, Grandpapa,' she teased, then added accusingly, 'You can't fool me. You're just afraid you won't get your sheep shorn in the Marshlands woolshed.'

'Nonsense,' Max snorted. 'Blair is a man of his word. He will not go back on it simply because he's annoyed by a girl with fire in her hair.'

She looked at him through troubled eyes. 'Grandy, please believe me when I say I've no wish to cause trouble between neighbours, but I can't allow that little boy to feel I'm rejecting him. Is it not possible for you to understand?'

He nodded gloomily. 'Of course I understand. I suppose you mean he'll feel he's being rejected *again*? We both know he's already been rejected by his mother.'

'Not entirely,' Lynn defended. 'Delphine has asked me to give her a report on the boy. She's anxious to know about his progress, and how he's faring without her.'

'Then you'll be able to tell her he's faring very well indeed while living in the homestead with Mrs Bates and the girl Sandra to care for him. I doubt that he's missing Delphine at all.'

'Perhaps you're right,' she said sadly, although she knew this to be untrue. Tony had come to see her because he had thought she could possibly be his mother.

It meant he had not forgotten Delphine, even if he had ceased his earlier fretting for her. However, Lynn had no wish for further discussion on the topic, therefore she said, 'I must go to the Waipawa supermarket tomorrow. I can't make wholemeal scones without wholemeal.'

In the meantime the evening meal waited to be prepared, and as she scrubbed the season's new potatoes her thoughts turned to Blair Marshall. Was it her imagination, or had he really kissed her while standing at this same bench? The memory of his enfolding arms holding her so closely against his body caused her breath to quicken, and she found herself gazing sightlessly through the window above the kitchen sink, her hands motionless.

But suddenly she pulled herself together. Snap out of it, stupid, she warned mentally. Don't let it go to your head. It doesn't mean a thing, especially to *him*—and no doubt he's offered the same treatment to every girl in the district.

This last thought irritated her to the extent of causing her to throw a potato into the saucepan with more force than necessary. Yet, pausing to think again, she felt that this Don Juan image did not really fit the character of Blair Marshall. A man of stability, Grandy had said.

Next day Lynn did not leave for the Waipawa township quite as early as she had intended. First the cottage had to be tidied, and then time was spent in drafting a story for teenagers. The idea had come to her during the first hours of awakening, and she knew the importance of anchoring it on paper before it vanished from her mind.

Lunch was then prepared, and, later, while Max enjoyed a short rest before leaving for his club, she wrote to Delphine. So far there had been little to report apart from the facts that the boy was being well cared for and appeared to be contented.

As she sealed the letter she heard the approach of the school bus. She held her breath, waiting for it to stop, but when it continued to rumble on its way she knew that Tony had not decided to pay her another visit. At least, not today.

A short time later she was driving her own blue Honda towards the small town which had been built on the banks of the Waipawa River. Its distance from the cottage was little more than two miles, and she had almost reached it when she saw Tony walking along the footpath in the direction of his home.

She reduced speed to watch him, noticing that he dawdled slowly while pausing to gaze at anything that caught his interest. Then, as she drew to the kerbside, his face lit when he saw who was in the car.

'Hi, Lynn!' he shouted, his relief evident.

She leaned over and opened the passenger door for him to get in. 'What are you doing here? Why didn't you get on the bus?'

'I missed it.'

'Surely the teacher didn't keep you in?'

'No, I was watching a fight.' His eyes shone at the memory as he rushed on to explain, 'When we came out of school two of the big boys started punching each other. All the other kids made a ring round them. Everyone was shouting until two teachers came out to make them stop. When I got to the gate the bus had gone, so now I've gotta walk home.'

She looked at him thoughtfully. 'I think you had better come with me. I've a letter to post and a few groceries to buy in the supermarket, and then I'll take you home.'

A short drive took her to the parking area of the supermarket, where she collected various items from the shelves while Tony pushed the shining nickel-plated trolley. Then, with the purchases locked in the car, they walked to the post office where she cleared her grandfather's mailbox and posted the letter to Delphine.

To reach this building they went through a garden-filled Centre Court which was surrounded by shops and edged by a children's play area. Tony trotted happily beside her, his unconcealed exuberance making her wonder if a trip to town was a rare treat for him, and she was still pondering this question as they made their way back across the Centre Court.

But suddenly he gave a gleeful shout as he left her side and ran towards a tall man who had emerged from the Bank of New Zealand on the far side of the Court. His voice reached her ears. 'Uncle Blair, Uncle Blair—I'm with Lynn.'

Blair stood still, waiting for her to reach his side. The scowl on his face indicated his anger while his tight jaw seemed to jut at her as he gritted, 'So, you took it upon yourself to bring the boy to town.'

'Not exactly——' she began.

'Collected him from the school, did you?' he rasped accusingly.

'Again, not exactly,' she said, her anger rising.

'Is it not possible for you to use your intelligence in this affair? Have you no wits at all?'

'How dare you speak to me in this manner?' she hissed furiously.

'I thought I'd made my wishes more than clear——'

'Your wishes do not concern me, Mr Marshall. I shall do as I think fit, and without any consultation with you.'

His mouth tightened as he said coldly, 'A silent worker, are you? Is this what your grandfather meant when he referred to your plans and activities? I recall you were very cagey about divulging what he meant. Do they involve a certain party?' His grey eyes, as bleak as granite, glanced down at the boy.

However, the reply Lynn was about to snap at him was forestalled by Tony tugging at Blair's coat. Looking up, he said plaintively, 'Uncle Blair, I'm *starving*.'

Blair's tone was still cool. 'Are you telling me you weren't fed on scones and jam today?'

Tony shook his head dolefully.

Blair's tone became dry. 'That's a shocking state of affairs. Do you think you could cope with a milk shake?'

Tony nodded vigorously. 'Yes, *please*, and one for Lynn, too?'

Lynn spoke hastily. 'No, thank you—it would choke me.'

Blair ignored the remark. 'We'll go to the restaurant and Miss Nichols will join me in a cup of tea.'

'That's what you think,' she snapped.

His face remained unsmiling. 'I already owe you a cup of tea. I intend to repay it right now while having a word in your ear about bringing this boy to town. You don't seem to have got the message.'

'Suppose I refuse to come to the restaurant?'

'Then I'll be interested to see if you put on a performance of kicking and yelling while I carry you there. It'll be the talk of the town.'

The dimple beside her mouth flickered at him. 'You're a positive tyrant, Mr Marshall. Did you learn your domineering ways from your cousin Stan?'

He scowled. 'Are you coming to have tea without a fuss?'

'Thank you, Mr Marshall. Perhaps it will help me cope with the wrath that is about to descend upon me.'

CHAPTER FOUR

BLAIR led them to a nearby restaurant where he ordered
a pot of tea, sandwiches, a milk shake and a cream bun
for Tony. He watched while Lynn filled their cups, then
commented in a sardonic tone, 'Your hand is shaking.
Why is that? Do you feel nervous—or guilty?'

It was true, she realised. Her hand was unsteady, but
his remark was sufficient to bring control of her nerves.
Her eyes swept a look of disdain over the man sitting
opposite her, and her chin rose as she said, 'Your sarcasm
doesn't even move me, Mr Marshall—therefore I shall
ignore it.'

His expression remained icy. 'But I do not intend to
ignore the fact that you've brought this boy to town.'

'As it happened I had a few purchases to make, and
I must say it doesn't appear to be an everyday occur-
rence for him.'

'So you decided to give him a treat,' he snapped,
making no attempt to conceal his anger. 'You're already
aware of my request regarding your association with him.
Do I have to spell it out again?'

'Spell it out as often as you wish,' she retorted. 'I am
not bound by your requests.' Then, sending a smile across
the table, she asked, 'What makes you imagine your
wishes are my priority?'

'It's not so much my wishes that are at stake—it's what
is best for a certain party,' he pointed out with infinite
patience.

'And you think that doesn't concern me?'

'What is best for the boy doesn't seem to have got
through to you, Miss Nichols.'

'You're completely wrong,' she snapped impatiently. 'I do have his interests at heart. Besides, I did come along at the right time.'

'What's that supposed to mean?'

'Oh, nothing much.' Loath to make an explanation, she brushed the question aside, then smiled inwardly as Tony began to make things clear.

Busy with his milk shake, he made loud gurgling noises at the end of his straw in the bottom of the glass, then looked up and spoke with suppressed excitement. 'Uncle Blair, I saw a fight today.'

The dark brows rose as the grey eyes questioned Lynn. 'What does he mean? Has old Max shown violence?'

Laughter escaped her. 'No, my presence has not yet antagonised him to that extent. Unlike some people I could name, he has not yet indicated that he'd prefer I was on my way home to Wellington.'

He glared at her in silence, obviously searching for a suitable answer, but before he could find one Tony's voice piped up with an explanation.

'It was at school, Uncle Blair. Two big boys punched and kicked each other. They rolled on the ground and got all muddy because it had been raining, and all the kids stood round to watch. Some of the girls began to cry. One girl hit them with her schoolbag.' The memory caused his eyes to become round.

'A real ding-dong, by the sound of it,' Blair commented. 'I presume it took place at what's commonly known as *playtime*?'

'No, it was after school,' Tony continued. 'Two teachers came out to pull the boys apart, then told everyone to go home.'

'Which included you,' Blair commented.

Tony nodded as he bit into his cream bun.

'I must admit to being slightly puzzled,' Blair went on. 'How did you happen to witness this bout of fisticuffs if you were on the school bus? I know it leaves the moment school comes out.'

Tony gave vent to his indignation. 'It didn't wait for me. When I got to the gate it had gone. Uncle Blair, you've gotta tell that bus driver he's gotta wait for me——'

'Especially if you're watching a fight. I'm afraid you'll have to take that as a lesson, old chap. The bus—like time and tide—waits for no man.' He paused while frowning thoughtfully at the boy. 'So what did you do?'

'I started to walk home.'

'A long trek at a snail's pace,' Lynn put in.

Tony said, 'And then Lynn saw me. She stopped her car and I got in and we went to the supermarket for groceries.'

'Wholemeal for scones,' Lynn murmured, sending an amused glance towards the nonplussed expression on Blair's face.

Tony concluded, 'And we posted a letter, and then we saw you, and you brought us here. Uncle Blair, I want to go out to the swings and the slide.'

'OK, off you go, but don't leave the play area until we come to fetch you,' Blair commanded as the boy slid from his seat and vanished through the door.

Lynn watched Blair stare into his cup, his brow now creased by a thoughtful frown. And, while she longed to release the laughter bubbling below the surface, instinct warned that this would be unwise. She knew that most men hated to be laughed at, and she doubted that Blair would be an exception. Besides, it would only give him further reason to be mad with her. Nevertheless, she said sweetly, 'Light is about to seep through the murkiness of your wrong conclusions and unjust suspicions, Mr Marshall?'

His tone became accusing. 'You knew about the fight. Why didn't you tell me you'd found him walking home?'

'Because it would have been so disappointing for you,' she said, smiling.

'Disappointing? What the devil do you mean?' The words were snapped crisply.

'It would have denied you further reason to be cross with me.'

'I still don't know what you're talking about.'

'Don't you realise that every time we've met you've found reason to be annoyed with me? It would be a pity to break the pattern.'

His expression betrayed amusement as he pointed out mockingly, 'I seem to recall a few moments yesterday when my annoyance appeared to have evaporated slightly.'

Her cheeks became pink as she found difficulty in meeting his eyes while recalling those same moments when his arms had held her against him. Nevertheless her face remained serious as she sent him a direct look, and although it was an effort to keep her voice steady she spoke calmly. 'That was merely your over-inflated ego at work, Mr Marshall. Like so many men you imagine you can kiss a girl whenever the whim strikes you. Well, I suppose there's a first and a last time for most things.'

'Are you offering me a dare?' he asked softly. 'Is it possible you'd like a repeat of yesterday's performance?'

She was startled by the suggestion. 'No, certainly not.'

'I didn't notice too much protest on your part,' he drawled.

'That was only because I decided to let you get it over and done with,' she retorted haughtily. 'Besides, how could I possibly struggle against the strength of your grip?'

'You mean when I held you closely against my body? If memory serves me correctly, that was when I felt your lips move beneath mine,' he jeered softly. 'Why can't you be honest and admit you loved every minute of it?'

'Because there's nothing to admit,' she lied in a cold voice, at the same time feeling a hypocrite. She had enjoyed his kisses and the feel of his arms about her, but was not yet ready to acknowledge this fact, not even to herself.

A smile played about his sensuous lips, then his eyes narrowed as he surveyed her. 'I can see there's only one course to take. Next time I'll have to put more effort into the experiment.'

'*Experiment?* Is that what it was?' Her voice echoed indignation. 'What makes you think you can experiment with me? Doesn't it matter to you if my emotions become involved?' Her lips curled as she went on disdainfully. 'Really, you're exactly like Stan.'

His tone became curt. 'Explain yourself. How am I like my cousin?'

'Your attitudes towards women appear to be very similar. Stan couldn't care less how much he hurt Delphine, while you—obviously—couldn't care less how much you hurt me.' Her voice held a faint tremor caused by a small lump in her throat.

'City girls appear to be perfectly capable of climbing over emotional obstacles,' he commented nonchalantly.

'That's what *you* think,' she snapped, thoroughly irritated. 'If I were not so...so *uninterested*, I might even begin to *hate* you.' But this, she knew, was untrue. He might dislike her, and indeed appeared to do so, but she could never hate him.

He gave a light laugh. 'Is that so? I trust you're not forgetting that hate is akin to love?' The last words came silkily.

A derisive laugh escaped her. 'Love, Mr Marshall? Men who think only of themselves know little of love.'

His mouth tightened while a muscle flexed in his cheek. 'Considering that you know so little about me, Miss Nichols, you're not in a position to judge whether or not I know anything of love.'

'Nor have I any wish to be in such a position,' she returned smoothly. Then, glancing at her watch, she added, 'Thank you for the tea, but it really is time I went home. Dare I ask if you'd like me to take Tony with me—or would you prefer to remove him from my doubtful company?'

He ignored her ironic tone as he queried, 'You'd take him straight to the homestead?'

'Naturally.'

'Then I'd be grateful if you'd do so. I have an appointment with my accountant.'

'Which would make coping with a small boy difficult—and which also means you don't mind his being with me when it suits you. May I suggest you phone from your accountant's office to make sure he has definitely been returned to Marshlands?'

'I doubt that it'll be necessary,' he informed her gravely, then, raising one dark brow, he queried, 'Is it your habit to keep your indignation on the boil?'

She forced a smile. 'Only when people are continually antagonistic towards me. And distrustful as well. I'm inclined to take umbrage when people look upon even my simplest actions with suspicion. So, shall we go?'

'Yes. I dislike being late for appointments. And thank you for taking care of Tony this afternoon——'

'Mr Marshall—you positively amaze me.'

He ignored her tone. 'I'll see you later,' he said casually.

These words also surprised her. 'Oh? When will that be?'

'Possibly this evening. You're right when you say there's antagonism between us. It's like a black cloud hanging over our heads—a cloud that should be swept away.'

His statement caused her spirits to lift. 'How do you propose to remove it?' she asked lightly.

'By trying to know you better. I see no reason why we shouldn't be *friends*.'

Friends being the operative word, she decided, noting his emphasis. Was this his way of telling her he was fancy-free and intended to remain in that happy state? Well, that made two of them because she also intended to remain fancy-free—or so she told herself. And then his next words continued to surprise her.

Casually, he said, 'This evening I shall take you out— that's if you'll accompany me, of course.'

She looked at him wordlessly, waiting to hear more.

'We'll go to the opening of a local arts and crafts exhibition. I'm a member, although not an active one, and I may take a guest. Will you come?'

'Yes, thank you. It sounds interesting.'

'Good. I'll call for you at seven forty-five.'

They left the restaurant and walked to where the nearby playground equipment was surrounded by lawns. The sound of squeaky swings rang on the air, and while some children swept back and forth others spun in circles of various-sized roundabouts.

They discovered Tony climbing the steps for yet another slither down the long slide. His dark hair blew in the wind, and when he reached the bottom Blair called to him, 'You've had a fair innings, old chap. You're going home now—with Lynn.'

She held her breath. He'd actually called her Lynn. It must have been a slip of the tongue. She then watched as he strode away.

The drive from town took only a short time, and as they drew near the Marshlands entrance Tony looked at her with eyes full of appeal. 'I don't want to go home. I want to go to your place.'

She stared straight ahead. 'Sorry, Tony. I promised Uncle Blair I'd take you home. Besides, hasn't he said you're not to go there?'

Tony nodded. 'Last night he sat on my bed and said that Frog Hollow is a dangerous place for little boys—and for big boys too.'

Lynn slanted an oblique glance towards the boy. 'He said that?'

Tony nodded again, this time vigorously. 'He said that sometimes ladies with red hair are really witches—and you've gotta run for your life.'

A surge of indignation assailed Lynn. 'Are you sure he said that?'

'Course I'm sure. And he said they're real bad if they've got green eyes that go all sparkly when the sun shines on them.' He turned to regard her seriously. 'Are you really a witch, Lynn?'

'Do I look like one?'

'No.' He thought about it then said, 'All the witches in my books have big noses and long teeth.'

'Who buys books for you? Daddy, I suppose?'

'No. Uncle Blair said it was time I had new ones. Sandra makes me keep them in my room. She says I gotta be tidy.'

Lynn said, 'I'd like to see your books. And your room,' she added as an afterthought. 'Do you think you could show them to me?'

'If—if Sandra will let me,' he said doubtfully.

'Then we'll just have to wait and see what sort of a reception you get. Something tells me that Sandra won't be particularly pleased with you.'

He caught the meaning of her words. 'She's going to be *real* mad with me. She's always a *bit* mad with me.'

Lynn did not pursue the subject. The last turn in the road had taken them up a short hill towards the Marshlands entrance where a cattle-grid was set in the ground between ornamental concrete pillars. Above it stretched the branches of oaks and elms, their gnarled trunks indicating they had been planted many years previously.

The metalled drive curved in a gradual rise towards the house on the hill, the green pastures on either side being grazed by ewes and lambs which scattered at the car's approach. Beyond the drive the homestead was a wide, two-storeyed timber-built structure, its white walls and contrasting deep blue roof giving it an air of distinction.

A second cattle-grid prevented livestock from entering the house enclosure, and after crossing it the drive skirted the front garden to sweep around to a spacious back yard edged by a vegetable garden.

Lynn followed the drive until she stopped the car near the steps of a back veranda. As she did so a door opened and two women emerged, one roundly built and middle-aged, while the other was blonde and not many years older than Lynn herself. Mrs Bates and Sandra Walsh, she thought, regarding them with interest.

Sandra hurried down the steps, her face pink, her prominent blue eyes flashing with anger as they glared through the driver's window at Lynn. 'I suppose you're old Max's granddaughter,' she hissed.

Lynn was taken aback. 'Yes, I am——'

'You've got a nerve,' Sandra went on. 'You know that little imp has been told he's not to go to Frog Hollow. Why didn't you bring him home before this late hour?'

Lynn took a grip on her patience. 'He hasn't been to Frog Hollow—at least not today.'

'You're lying,' Sandra accused loudly.

Lynn drew a sharp breath, her own anger rising. 'How dare you——?'

Maisie Bates hurried down the steps, a worried frown on her round face. 'Don't be too hasty, Sandra,' she advised. 'There could be a mistake—and you know you're very good at jumping to the wrong conclusion.' She smiled apologetically at Lynn. 'I'm afraid Sandra is inclined to become upset.'

Tony put in, 'Mrs Bates, I saw a fight. Two of the big boys——'

Sandra silenced him. 'Shut up, Tony. Just get out of that car and go inside at once.' Then, as Tony made no move to do so, she turned to Maisie Bates. 'Please see if you can get him out of the car. We don't want an exhibition of kicking and yelling while I try to get him out. Perhaps Bert would come and help.'

Lynn looked at her curiously. 'Why do you take this attitude with the boy? Are you always so unpleasant to him?'

'Yes, she is!' Tony shouted, then leaned towards Lynn as though seeking protection from the wrath hanging over his head.

Lynn decided it was time she told Maisie about how and where she had met Tony, and as she did so the boy left his seat in the car and moved to stand beside the older woman. Looking up into her face he said, 'Mrs Bates, I want to show Lynn my books. I want to show her where I sleep.'

Sandra's voice cut in sharply. 'Certainly not—we don't allow strangers into this house.'

Her words brought a storm of tearful protest from Tony.

Lynn made an effort to comfort him. She regretted that the request had ever been made, and she now said, 'It doesn't matter, Tony. Perhaps there'll be another opportunity.'

But this suggestion did not satisfy Tony, who sat on the veranda steps and began to sob piteously.

The sight of his anguish was too much for Maisie Bates, who gave a resigned sigh as she said, 'Very well— I doubt that it can do any harm, and we must have peace at any price.' Then she smiled at Lynn as she added, 'Come with me. I'm sure Blair won't mind. He's a very understanding man, as you've probably noticed for yourself.'

Have I? Lynn wondered. At the moment she wasn't sure what she felt about Blair Marshall, although she realised there was something about him that made her pulses quicken.

She left the car and followed Maisie into a kitchen which needed only a glance to show it was equipped with almost every modern appliance. A door from it led into the thickly carpeted hall, and from there they went up the stairs. Tony raced ahead, his tears having miraculously vanished while he chattered with excitement, and Sandra lagged behind in sulky silence.

At the top of the stairs a hall ran the length of the house, and as Maisie ushered Lynn into one of the rooms leading from it she said, 'This is where Tony sleeps. I understand it has always been known as the nursery, although there have been precious few children in it for many years. That rocking-horse belonged to Blair's grandfather and later to his father and aunts. It's really an antique.'

'Stan must be the son of one of Blair's aunts,' Lynn mused.

'That's right. He's Blair's oldest cousin,' Maisie informed her. 'Are you saying you know him?'

'I've met him,' Lynn admitted briefly, then changed the subject by turning her attention to the large dapple-grey rocking-horse with its arched neck, cream mane and tail, and its red saddle complete with small stirrups. 'It's a beauty,' she said, causing it to move backward and forward on its swingers. 'Can you ride it, Tony?'

'Course I can ride it,' he declared indignantly, scrambling up to its high back and proceeding to rock vigorously. 'It's name is Dobbin, and see—it has a saddlebag too.'

Maisie said, 'Only heaven knows when future riders for it will appear—but I'm afraid the thought of marriage has little or no interest for Blair.'

Lynn was not to be drawn by Maisie's remark. Instead she spoke to the boy. 'You promised to show me your books, Tony.'

He ceased his strenuous rocking and clambered down from Dobbin. 'I have to keep them over here,' he said, leading her towards a bookcase on the other side of the room.

Sandra spoke acidly. 'See that you leave them in a tidy stack. We can't have the room in a continual shambles.'

'He's only a little boy,' Maisie protested. 'Sometimes I think you're too hard on him.'

'He must be disciplined,' Sandra retorted acidly.

'He's had so much to contend with,' Maisie went on. 'What with his mother leaving him and now his father away on holiday——'

'He appears to be surviving,' Sandra pointed out coldly.

'That's because he still has Uncle Blair to care for him,' Lynn said, pausing in the examination of one of Tony's books. 'No doubt his uncle feels responsible for him.'

'Which is why he has forbidden Tony to go near Frog Hollow,' Sandra put in. 'I trust you're well aware of that fact.' The blue eyes held a cold glint as they stared at Lynn.

But Lynn scarcely heard her. A photo which had inadvertently become lodged between the books now fell to the floor, and as she bent to pick it up she realised it was one of the casual photos taken at Delphine and Stan's wedding. The smiling Delphine looked happy, while Stan wore a satisfied grin. Beside them stood Lynn herself, her cloud of red hair complemented by the green dress she had bought for the occasion.

Sandra saw her staring at the photo. 'Is that thing still lying about the place?' she said crossly. 'It's got his mother in it. I'll put it out of sight.'

There was a shriek from Tony. 'No! No! It's mine——'

Maisie spoke sharply. 'You will leave it alone, Sandra. It belongs to the boy. And, what's more, I think it's time you attended to his meal.'

Tony spoke loudly. 'I'm not going to eat *spinach* or *carrots*——'

'You'll eat what's given to you,' Sandra snapped as she flounced from the room.

Lynn watched her go then turned to Maisie. 'Is she always so cross?'

The older woman gave a small apologetic smile. 'I try to make allowances for Sandra because I suspect she's frustrated. I think she's keen on a certain party but appears to be getting nowhere.'

Lynn's brows rose as the obvious question leapt into her mind. 'Do you mean she has hopes of becoming emotionally involved with . . . ?'

'With Blair? Oh, no. As I said, he doesn't appear to be looking at anyone.' Then, lowering her voice, she whispered, 'The poor girl seems to have set her heart on Gary Palmer, who works here, but he treats her so *casually*.'

The mention of Blair caused Lynn to recall that she was going out with him that evening. She also realised she must do something about her hair, therefore she glanced at her watch and said, 'I must go home, otherwise my grandfather will think I've left for parts unknown.'

'Just like the boy's mother,' Maisie said in a voice too low for Tony to hear. 'However, I've yet to see a marriage breakup where there aren't faults on both sides, although the female usually gets the worst of it.'

Tony, who had caught her last words, looked up at Lynn. 'What's a female?' he asked.

She smiled at him, then said impulsively, 'I'm sure Uncle Blair will be able to explain. He'll probably tell you it's rather like a witch,' she added as they went downstairs.

During the drive home Lynn memorised details of the nursery, the focal point which kept leaping into her mind being the rocking-horse. But instead of seeing Tony swing back and forth she visualised a juvenile Blair riding gleefully to wherever his little boy's imagination was taking him.

And then she recalled Maisie's remark that heaven alone knew where the future riders would come from. Blair appeared to have little thought of marriage, she had said.

So what of it? Lynn asked herself. It didn't mean he lived the life of a recluse, and suddenly the thought of Blair with other women set off a whirl of strange turbulence in her mind. It was enough to warn her of the danger looming ahead if she allowed her own emotions to become involved.

When she reached home she moved quickly to prepare the evening meal, then, after showering with rollers in her hair, came the problem of knowing what to wear. Nothing too formal for an arts and crafts exhibition, she thought, eventually deciding upon a woollen skirt and top in pale apricot, and as she attached her gold earrings she heard Max open the door to Blair.

She sent a last glance towards the mirror before going out to meet him, then, as she surveyed his handsome appearance, she became vitally conscious of the male aura that seemed to reach out and touch her. It was enough to send her pulses racing.

Blair looked at her for several moments, his eyes betraying a glint of admiration as they took in the way she had done her hair, and the curves beneath the subtle draping of the apricot top. But all he said was, 'You'll need a wrap of some kind.'

'I have this.' She lifted a cream handwoven cape from a chair.

He took it from her, placed it about her shoulders, then attended to the diagonal fastening of buttons. As he did so his expression remained grave.

Looking up, Lynn found herself unable to drag her eyes away from his face, and she was also aware that her grandfather watched them both with interest. It was almost as if Grandy expected Blair to kiss her, she thought, and confirmation of this came when the old man whispered in her ear, 'Don't forget to tell him about Queen of the Frogs.'

Fortunately Blair had gone ahead to open the door of his grey Peugeot, and this fact enabled Lynn to say in a low voice, 'Will you please stop jumping to conclusions, Grandy?'

The journey to the exhibition took less than ten minutes, and as they drove through the darkness Blair told her a little about the society, which had been formed twenty years previously. The sound of his deep voice was pleasant in her ears, causing her to wish the journey could have been much longer.

'It functions in an old school consisting of four large rooms and a central hall,' he told her. 'They have equipment such as kilns, pottery wheels and easels for oil-painters, although I understand the spinners take their own spinning wheels.'

'You appear to know a great deal about it,' she remarked.

'Only through Maisie Bates. She's a member of the wool group and is sure to be here this evening.'

There would be nothing to make the evening wildly exciting, Lynn realised, yet she was more than aware of the exhilaration growing within herself. And while she tried to tell herself its cause lay in the fact that this would be something *different* for her, honesty forced her to admit that it was because Blair Marshall had invited her to attend the function with him. After all, there must be numerous others he could have asked to accompany him, but instead—he had chosen her.

The old school proved to be a high-gabled timber building, its red paint and white facings showing up in the blaze of light streaming from every window. A large number of cars were parked in the vicinity, and after finding a space among them Blair took her arm while they crossed the road towards the entrance.

The pressure of his hand caused her breath to quicken, and although she felt the colour in her cheeks deepen, she was unaware that his touch was causing her eyes to sparkle. Nor was she conscious of the people who turned to stare as they entered the hall, nor of the eyes that were full of curiosity.

They found the rooms filled with people, who chatted as they sipped wine while examining the numerous exhibits of paintings, knitted and woven garments, ceramics, pottery, patchwork and porcelain dolls. Blair seemed to know so many of them, introducing her to people whose names she was unable to remember, and it was while admiring the array of patchwork quilts that a hand on her arm caused her to turn to find Maisie Bates standing beside her.

Brown eyes smiled into her own as Maisie whispered, 'Several people have asked me who you are.'

Lynn felt startled. 'Oh? Why should I interest them?'

'Because you look so lovely, and because you're with *him*, of course. He knows so many women, but doesn't make a habit of taking them out. It's almost as if he has you on show.'

'His own personal exhibit?' Lynn queried with a laugh, her eyes resting upon Blair, who had stepped aside to converse with friends. Dressed in formal clothes, he looked so handsome that she felt proud to be with him, and again she felt something stirring within her.

Maisie's tone became confidential as she laid a hand on Lynn's arm. 'My dear, most of these people know he's an eligible bachelor, therefore they can't help being interested.'

'It's possible they also know that he's allergic to city girls, therefore they'll not make too much of it,' Lynn returned.

Blair rejoined them at that moment and, looking at Maisie, he said, 'I'd like you to show Lynn your own work.'

Maisie looked pleased as she said modestly, 'Oh, well . . . there's nothing special about it.'

They returned to the wool room where the knitted and woven garments were displayed, and where red spots on labels indicated that several of Maisie's caps, scarves and shawls had already been sold. All the work was in the varied greys and creams of the natural wool, and Lynn was unable to resist buying one of Maisie's Fair Isle caps for her grandfather. And then her attention was caught by a fluted bed-cape, knitted in finely spun cream wool. She visualised it about her mother's shoulders; therefore, to Maisie's delight she purchased it.

Blair looked smug as he said, 'You could make all these things for yourself, if you learn to spin. I'm sure Maisie would teach you. She has taught several people—isn't that so, Maisie?' The dark brows were raised as he turned to her.

Maisie's brown eyes widened to betray her surprise. 'Yes, of course I'd teach you—in fact it would give me much pleasure to do so. I have a spare wheel I could lend you, and there's plenty of wool.'

'Especially with shearing just round the corner,' Blair put in. 'Max would be delighted to see his grand-daughter spinning wool from his own sheep.'

Lynn said nothing as she looked from Maisie's smiling face to Blair's enigmatic expression. She had the un-comfortable sensation of being suddenly bulldozed into an activity to which she had given no previous thought, and she also knew that her spare time must be devoted to her manuscripts. However, she had no wish to give a blunt refusal, and therefore she was thankful when the arrival of coffee and savouries enabled her to side-step the issue.

They drove home a short time later, and as they turned the corners of the quiet country road it became clear that the question still hovered in Blair's mind. 'Well, what did you think of the exhibition?' he asked casually when they had almost reached Frog Hollow.

'To be honest, I was amazed by the quality and variety of the work,' she admitted.

'All achieved by country women,' he pointed out drily. 'Some of them living away out in the backblocks.' As he spoke he reduced speed, drew to the wide grassy verge of the road and switched off the motor.

The action caused her to send him a glance of surprise. They were still a short distance from home, and it seemed as if he intended to take her in his arms, and while waiting for him to do so her heart began to thump.

But instead of reaching towards her he merely twisted in his seat and turned to face her. 'All women should have a hobby of some sort,' he said.

She remained silent, realising he had more to say on this subject. Nor was she mistaken.

'You can see the scope that was open to Delphine,' he went on. 'Despite her academic tendencies she could have learned new skills.'

'Yes, I can see what you mean,' she said quietly, while pushing the feeling of anticlimax from her. Then she turned to face him squarely as she asked, 'Is this why you took me to that exhibition this evening? Was it to show me what Delphine could have done?'

'Not exactly.' He hesitated, then admitted, 'I was really hoping to show you what you yourself could do.'

She felt puzzled. 'For what reason?'

He looked away from her, staring into the darkness beyond the windscreen. 'Because I think you should become interested in some of these activities enjoyed by country women.'

'Aren't you forgetting I'll be going home to Wellington?'

'The call of the city is loud and clear?' His tone was sardonic.

'Not yet. I've been too busy to hear even a whisper from it. Also, I like being with Grandy. I won't have him forever.'

He turned to face her again. 'Didn't he say you have a plan of some sort? Is that what keeps you so busy?'

She kept her voice cool. 'I suppose you could say so.'

'But you've no intention of telling me about it.'

She remained silent, disliking the direction in which the conversation was heading.

'Is there a great need to be so secretive?' he persisted.

'Why have you such a great need to learn about it?' she parried, realising that Grandy's remark about her having a plan had been most unfortunate. It had roused Blair's curiosity, and now her own reluctance to confide in him had caused suspicion to raise its head.

'Would it surprise you to know I'm wondering if it involves the boy?' he rasped.

'I've already told you that I intend sending Delphine a report,' she reminded him. 'Apart from that...' Her shoulders lifted in a slight shrug.

Why didn't she tell him about her other activities? she asked herself. The answer was plain enough. She feared his derision. If you *must* write, why not write for *adults*? he'd be sure to ask in a voice full of sarcasm. Or would that be beyond your capabilities?

And then the silence between them was broken as Blair's voice hit her ears. 'OK—I've got the message. You're telling me to mind my own damned business,' he gritted, switching on the motor.

The remainder of the journey home was completed in a tense silence which filled Lynn with dejection. She sensed that Blair was really annoyed with her, but, after all, what was so different about that? He'd been annoyed with her on several occasions, hadn't he?

When they reached Frog Hollow she sent him a wan smile as she said, 'Thank you for taking me to the exhibition. I enjoyed it.'

His response was as casual as it was cool. 'I'm glad Maisie had such good sales.'

The words seemed to tell Lynn that his thoughts were hardly with her, and that if she imagined she was about to be kissed she could think again. Then, as he made a move to open the car door for her, she forestalled him by lifting the handle and sliding from the seat. By the time she reached the veranda the car had already been backed on to the road and was heading away with a flare of red tail-lights.

Later, as she lay in her bed, she was overwhelmed by an acute disappointment. She had looked forward to going out with him this evening. She had hoped she would be kissed, she acknowledged to herself. She had longed to feel the strength of his arms about her, but not one of these things had happened. Instead, the furthering of an amicable relationship had ended in disaster.

Even more disturbing was the fact that his irritation seemed to be mingled with distrust—and that distrust had evolved from a casual word let fall by Grandy. For heaven's sake, what *plan* could Blair imagine she had in mind? Lynn wondered, her mind in a state of confusion.

CHAPTER FIVE

NEXT morning Lynn made an effort to brush all thoughts of Blair Marshall from her mind. She wasted no time while putting the cottage in order, and the moment her grandfather had left to walk round his flock of black ewes and lambs she began another letter to Delphine. She now had more definite information concerning the circumstances in which Tony was living, and she was anxious to record the details while they were still fresh in her memory.

It was easy enough to tell Delphine about Maisie Bates, from whom Tony could expect kindness, although her mention of Sandra was kept deliberately vague. However, when she tried to tell her about Blair Marshall, her fingers faltered above the keys of the typewriter. And while his handsome face with its dark grey eyes hovered in her mind, she was unable to find words that would not betray her own growing interest in him.

Soon her thoughts became a dizzy whirl of questions she was unable to answer, and it was almost lunchtime before she was able to seal the letter. As she did so she became conscious of a feeling of relief which almost amounted to a sense of freedom. It was as if she had discharged a debt that had weighed heavily on her mind, and she felt there was little more she could do for Delphine, apart from taking a photo of Tony and sending it to her.

Later, as she drove to the township to post the letter, she was forced to admit that her sympathies had undergone a subtle change. They were no longer so strongly with Delphine, but had now switched entirely to the boy, and she found herself becoming increasingly critical of her friend.

Despite her marital problems with Stan, how could Delphine have left her child to the mercy of other people? How could she have shelved her responsibilities by going so far away from him? She had been given access to him, so why couldn't she have remained in New Zealand where she could have at least kept a closer eye on him?

Lynn was still engrossed by these thoughts as she hurried into the post office, and in her haste she failed to see Blair before she had collided with him. His grip on her arm saved her from overbalancing, and as the letter slipped from her hand he bent to retrieve it.

A rapid glance revealed its destination. 'A weighty epistle to your friend, I see.' The comment was accompanied by a wry twist to his mouth.

She looked down at the letter. 'There seemed to be so much to tell her—but I think I've covered most of it.'

'Such as . . .?'

'Such as Maisie's kindness in knitting homespun jersies for him, and that lovely rocking-horse in the nursery, and . . . and the care you take of him,' she added, raking in her mind for a few details in the letter.

His eyes became hooded. 'You mean I actually get a mention?'

'Of course.'

'But only on account of the boy?'

She found herself unable to look at him, fearing that to do so would betray her growing interest. 'What other reason would there be?' she asked at last.

'Indeed—what other reason *could* there be?' he returned, the words being accompanied by a light laugh which had a mocking ring.

'Do you mind if I post it before the mail closes?' Her words held an exaggerated politeness.

'You do that, and then you can tell me more about your association with this woman whom my cousin married.'

'You mean the woman who sacrificed a pleasant career in Wellington for an unsatisfactory life at Marshlands,' she retorted.

'Preserve me from career-minded women,' he said wearily.

'I'm sure you'll be safe,' she snapped.

He ignored the remark as he prompted, 'You said she was with a publishing firm.'

'Yes. I met her at a time when I'd been bitten by the idea that it would be nice to write for children...' She stopped, annoyed with herself for uttering those last words.

He laughed, his amusement evident as his mind jumped to an obvious conclusion. 'Don't tell me—let me guess. You tried and they turned down your efforts.'

She looked away from him, maintaining an aloof silence. *Typical* of him to look upon her as a failure, she thought, controlling her irritation with difficulty.

He continued in a more kindly tone. 'One has to be persistent in these matters. One has to *try*, *try* again. There must be many thousands of unpublished manuscripts reposing in bottom drawers—forgotten and forlorn, and unlikely to see the light of day.'

'Probably millions of them,' she agreed sadly.

The sympathy in his voice deepened. 'Perhaps you could try again some day.'

She suppressed a smile. 'Yes—perhaps I could make further efforts.' Then, feeling a hypocrite, she went on hastily to tell him how she had brought Delphine to Frog Hollow, and of the romance that had developed. 'But it was all too rapid,' she finished sadly. 'Delphine married in haste—and repented at Marshlands.'

'Is that a fact?' He gave a short laugh, then regarded her thoughtfully before he said, 'Suppose you tell me more over a cup of tea. The restaurant is only a few steps away.'

Impulsively she suggested, 'Let's go home. It's my turn to provide the tea.'

He grinned. 'Only if there are wholemeal scones.'

'Baked just before lunch,' she assured him. 'I'll see you at Frog Hollow.'

She left him and made her way to where the Honda stood parked. Her step was light and her spirits rose for reasons she had no wish to examine, but as she switched on the ignition she wondered at the wisdom of the invitation.

Suppose they found Tony waiting for them? With Grandy at his club the boy would be alone—and in trouble because Blair would be furious with him. And then the delicate relations between Blair and herself would suffer another setback. The latter thought caused her to hold her breath as she arrived at the cottage, then a sigh of relief escaped her when there was no sign of the boy.

The electric kettle was put on, and by the time Blair stepped into the kitchen the tea had been made, the scones buttered and spread with raspberry jam. Did he recall how he had kissed her in this room? she wondered. Was memory of it the cause of the tight line now hovering about his mouth?

Making an effort to keep her thoughts on an even keel she said, 'There's a clean towel beside the basin, if you'd like to wash your hands.'

'Thank you.' He disappeared towards the bathroom, but when he returned his lips were still slightly compressed as he reverted to their former subject. 'So—what more is there to tell about Delphine?'

Her shoulders lifted in a vague shrug. 'Very little. In any case your tone indicates your complete lack of sympathy with her. I doubt that it's possible for you to see further than a man's view of any question.'

'You know nothing of my views,' he pointed out sharply.

She ignored the reprimand as she went on sweetly, 'Women are no longer the slaves of men, Mr Marshall. There's this thing called Women's Lib. The female of the species has asserted itself——'

'And become "more deadly than the male,"' he quoted.

She controlled her exasperation. 'Surely the female is now a more interesting mate for the male? Or do you consider her talents should remain dulled by kitchen chores while she attends to his stomach, his washing and ironing, and to his mending——?'

'And to sleeping with him,' he interrupted softly. 'Don't forget that most wives enjoy sleeping with their mates. They love attending to a man's deepest needs, but that is something you've yet to learn.'

Her cheeks began to feel warm as his meaning seeped into her mind. She found herself unable to look at him, and then his next words caused surprise.

'I'll confess that Stan has always been somewhat self-centred,' he admitted reluctantly.

'Heaven preserve me from such a man,' she emphasised with a touch of vehemence.

'Then you have to watch your step,' he advised in a serious tone. 'You must be careful to set your sights on a city fellow: someone who will be happy to see you rush away in the early morning, slave for somebody else all day, then wearily drag yourself home late in the evening. I presume that's what you have in mind for your own future?'

'No, it is not,' she retorted crossly.

'No? Then what do you visualise for yourself?' He smiled.

'That is not your concern,' she snapped, irritated by his obvious amusement.

'Surely you intend to marry sooner or later?'

'Really, I haven't given it a thought.'

'Then isn't it time you did so?' His eyes became penetrating. 'You must be twenty-three at least.'

'Actually, twenty-four. I was seventeen when I was Delphine's bridesmaid,' she told him, recalling the photo she had seen in the nursery at Marshlands.

'That makes you eight years my junior,' he conceded in a manner which made him sound almost fatherly.

'Then isn't it time that you yourself were married? Or haven't you found a suitable person who is willing to—to *toe the line*?'

He frowned. 'You seem to be determined to quarrel with me.'

'And you seem to be set on delving into my private affairs. I understood it was my association with Delphine you wished to discuss, rather than myself, Mr Marshall.'

A shade of impatience crossed his face. 'You know perfectly well that my name is Blair—therefore I'm warning you that the next time you call me Mr Marshall I shall kiss you.'

'In that case I'll take care not to offend again—Blair.'

'So, is there a strong reason why your plans for the future should not be discussed?'

Apprehension filled her as she sent him a rapid glance. 'My *plans*? Ah, we're back to that, are we?'

He went on unperturbed. 'Most girls of your age have ideas of overseas travel in mind. You've no thoughts of it at all?'

She laughed. 'My only travel plans consist of driving home to Wellington, although I haven't yet decided when that will be.'

'Good. Then I apologise for my apparent nosiness.' He regarded her in glum silence until he said, 'I must admit I feared you were in the process of hatching other...travel plans.'

Questions leapt into her eyes. 'You did? Such as what?'

'Well, travel tied up with the plans referred to by Max, and about which you've been so secretive.' He left the table to take a few restless paces about the room, then paused at the open back door to stare towards the water.

Watching him, she said, 'I'm afraid your imagination is running away with you—although I must say something appears to be really bugging you. Why don't you bring it out into the open?'

He swung round to face her. 'OK, I'll be frank with you. But first it might be possible for you to tell me why I'm plagued by a strong suspicion that there's more to your interest in the boy than meets the eye. I mean, something more than just sending a report on him,' he added as he returned to the table.

'Perhaps it's because you possess a suspicious mind. I've noticed it before. For instance, there were your suspicions concerning my relationship with Stan—and your suspicions that I was the cause of the marriage breakup.'

'Those thoughts no longer nag at me,' he informed her curtly.

'So now you've switched to suspecting I have an ulterior motive for befriending the boy? Is it a motive which includes travel plans?' she queried as a thought sprang into her head.

'It's possible,' he admitted, staring at her gloomily.

She drew a sharp breath as an inner hurt began to make itself felt, then she spoke quietly. 'Really—I had no idea your distrust of me ran so deeply. What do you imagine I have in mind? A plan to *kidnap him*?' Her tone had become scathing.

'Delphine wouldn't be the first separated parent to make such an arrangement.' His eyes had become narrowed and watchful. 'Is it possible she's now conniving for you to take the boy to her?'

Lynn gaped at him in shocked fury, then she exploded, 'Do you honestly believe I could be stupid enough to make such an attempt? Even if the request had come up, it's a task I couldn't handle. The first problem would be the matter of his passport.'

'Yes—of course.' Relief flooded his voice. 'Actually, I hadn't thought it through.'

Exasperated, her voice rose in further anger. 'It seems to me that your distrust is surpassed only by your low opinion of my intelligence, which means—Mr Marshall—that you must think I'm utterly and completely *daft*.'

A gleam appeared in his eyes. He replaced his cup on its saucer, left his seat and moved to her side of the table.

She sensed his intentions and cringed in her chair. Gripping the edge of the table she spat, 'Don't you dare touch me . . . don't you jolly well dare——'

'I warned you about this *Mr Marshall* business—and now you've asked for it.'

'I'll scream. I'm warning you, I'll scream——'

'You do that. Old Mick out there will think you're learning to bark. Or he might think it's the fire siren and join in the chorus.'

Her grip on the table tightened, but despite her efforts to avoid being embraced his strong arms dragged her out of her chair and held her against him. And, although she tried to whip herself into a frenzy of indignation, her struggles became half-hearted as his lips descended upon her own.

Nor was she able to deny the tingling pleasure surging through her nerves. And to make matters worse her pulses raced, her breath quickened as the kiss deepened, and, although she tried to steel herself against a response, her arms began to creep about his neck. She also knew that he guessed she was anything but unaffected, and this was proved when the kiss was broken while he looked down into her flushed face.

'You liked that,' he jeered in soft, mocking tones. 'You're longing for more.'

'Don't flatter yourself,' she gasped, feeling a denial was necessary. 'If I wanted more it wouldn't be from you.'

He laughed. 'Are you trying to hint it would be from somebody you've left in Wellington? Don't try to lie to me because I don't believe you.'

She glared at him coldly. 'Why shouldn't there be somebody in Wellington? I know lots of men in that city.'

'Of course you do,' he soothed. 'But I doubt that you'd leave anyone who is special for an indefinite period at Frog Hollow. And there's something else . . .'

'Oh? What would that be, Mr Know-all?'

'If a lover in Wellington filled your mind you wouldn't have returned my kiss.'

'That's a lie. I did not return your kiss.'

'No? Are you trying to convince me—or yourself? I was sure your lips parted the moment you knew you'd aroused me.'

She could only stare at him speechlessly, knowing that she had been conscious of the sensual call his arousal had sent to her own body, and of the response within herself.

He went on, 'Of course you were well aware that you were sending my blood up through the top of my head— and that you were doing other things to me as well. Do you deny it?'

'I-I don't know what you mean,' she prevaricated in a faint whisper, at the same time hiding her face against his shoulder.

'Come now—you're too mature to be quite so naïve. You're an adult and ready to be loved. In fact you're longing for it—and I'm well aware that you're fire below the surface.'

He bent his head and found her lips again, and, as one hand held her closely, the other clasped her breast before moving to knead the muscles along her spine. It

made its way slowly, creeping down towards her buttocks while the pressure of his body against her own
confirmed the quickening of his desire.

This time she gave up all thought of pretence. Her
arms crept up to encircle his neck, and as her fingers
entwined themselves in his hair her parted lips made no
secret of her response. But even as the world seemed to
stand still a surge of common sense caused her fingers
to pause in caressing the hair at his nape. She lowered
her arms, and, pushing with her hands against his chest,
a small gasp escaped her. 'Please...no more... I think
it's time you went home.'

'You're sure you want me to leave?' he murmured,
his arms making no effort to release her while his lips
nuzzled her ear before tracing a line to her throat.

'Yes...you must go. It's—it's time I made a start on—
on preparing the evening meal.' Her last words came
with a rush.

'Perhaps you're right—otherwise things might get out
of hand. Old Max will take umbrage if he comes home
to find his cook in bed with the neighbour, and no
evening meal ready.'

A shaky laugh escaped her, but it was cut short as a
voice spoke from behind them. 'Uncle Blair—is Lynn
your girlfriend?'

They froze, then turned to see Tony standing at the
open doorway, his hands clasping a small object.

Blair's features became stern. 'What are you doing
here? You're supposed to be at home.'

Tony squinted up at him, the late afternoon sun
glinting in his hazel eyes. 'I came to see Lynn. I came
to show her my frog. Look, Lynn—*I've gotta frog.*'

Lynn tried to lighten the situation. She peered closely
at the small green snout and bulbous eyes poking from
between Tony's fingers. 'I believe that's Freddie,' she
exclaimed.

'You *know* this frog?' Tony queried in an awed voice.

'I can't say we're close friends,' she admitted, then added with a smile, 'He's probably still searching for the tail he had when he was a tadpole.'

'Very annoying to lose a good tail,' Blair put in. 'You'd better let him get on with the job.'

Lynn said unthinkingly, 'Some day I'll tell you a story about Freddie Frog who took singing lessons, but now you'd better wash your hands and have——'

But Tony had already seen the scones on the table. The frog was released, and the boy ran to the bathroom.

During his absence Blair sent Lynn a rueful smile. 'Scones, stories—how can I persuade him to listen to my instructions when you put up such opposition?'

'Only by finding your own opposition,' she suggested.

'What would that be, may I ask? He has everything he needs at home, and I'm sure Maisie and Sandra are kind to him.'

'Oh, yes, I feel confident you can rely on Maisie,' she said, remembering the kindly round face of the housekeeper.

'But not on Sandra?' he queried sharply.

'I'm sure Sandra is doing her best according to her lights,' she said after a few moments of careful thought.

Tony returned in time to hear the last remark. 'Sandra says she doesn't like you,' he reported to Lynn. 'She told Uncle Blair you went nosing upstairs.'

Lynn's brows rose as she turned anxious eyes upon Blair. 'Did she really tell you that? I hope you didn't believe her.'

He shrugged. 'Do you imagine I took any notice of her?'

'How would I know? It's possible you believe every word she says.'

'You must think I'm idiotic. Maisie assured me it was Tony's idea to show you his books and where he sleeps.'

Tony piped up, 'And I showed Lynn how well I can ride Dobbin. Uncle Blair, when can I have a *real* pony?'

'That'll be for your father to decide, old chap.'

'Do you think he'll come back and get one for me?' Tony looked at Blair anxiously.

'Of course he'll come back,' Blair assured him. 'He's merely taking a holiday.'

The boy's eyes still held questions as he said, 'Sandra says he won't come home if I don't eat every vegetable on my plate. Sandra says he'll be like my mother and stay away forever.'

'I'll have a word in Sandra's ear,' Blair promised grimly. 'Now then, you will thank Lynn for her hospitality, and you will set off for home—up the zigzag at a gallop.'

'Like on a real pony,' Tony said gleefully. He wiped his mouth with the back of his hand then flung his arms about Lynn. 'Thank you for the nice jammy scones!'

The impulsive gesture touched her, and as she hugged Tony she dropped a light kiss on his forehead. A few minutes later she watched from the doorway as he ran towards the hillside track, then she turned to Blair with an anxious question. 'Do you think he's old enough to have a pony?'

'Of course he's old enough. At this age I was jumping at pony club.' A smile crossed his face while a gleam of triumph lit the grey eyes. 'I believe that's the answer.'

'The answer to what?'

'To the question of opposition. A pony of his own could solve the problem of competing with the attractions at Frog Hollow. A pony would get him off the school bus in double-quick time, and that would be a relief to us all.'

'Yes, indeed, a great relief...'

'Naturally, he'll need supervision, and that's where Sandra will shine. She rides really well.'

'She goes riding with you?' The question came casually.

'No, but there are occasions when she rides over the farm with Gary. She keeps her own horse on the place.' He paused, then sent her a glance of enquiry. 'Do you ride, Lynn?'

'No, I'm afraid not. A mere city girl, you understand.'

'Oh, yes—I'd almost forgotten that important fact.' Something that was almost a sigh escaped him as he went on, 'I shall begin searching for a suitable mount for a beginner. They're not easy to find.' His strong even teeth flashed as he sent her a teasing grin. 'Are you ready to recognise defeat?'

She looked at him blankly. 'Defeat? What are you talking about?'

'I'm saying that you'd better get ready to learn that a pony will overshadow anything that Frog Hollow has to offer. Even scones and raspberry jam and loving hugs from you.'

'You're really exaggerating the situation,' she informed him in a lofty tone. 'Please believe I'll be more than satisfied to see Tony in a happy state of mind—wherever he happens to be.'

'Is it possible you consider that place is with his mother?'

The question startled her. 'I did not say that, but if you want my honest opinion I think his mother would give him love.'

'Your honest opinion,' he mused. 'Are you always honest, Lynn?'

'You have your doubts about it?' she queried coolly.

He moved to stand before her, his gaze searching as he took her face between his hands. 'Tell me truly—was your response to my kisses completely honest?'

'As sincere as your own kisses,' she prevaricated, returning his scrutiny without flinching although the feel of his hands was sending a tremor through her.

They remained motionless for several long moments before he lowered his head to brush his lips across her forehead, her cheekbones, and lastly the dimple beside her mouth. Then he left her standing in a daze while he strode through the living-room and across the front veranda.

She heard the rev of the motor as the car was backed towards the road, and even after the sound had faded she remained still, gazing into space until she whispered audibly, 'Blair Marshall—you really are a man to contend with.'

Her fingers touched her face gently, and, while she knew she should press a cold wet cloth to her face before Grandy walked in the door, she was reluctant to wipe away Blair's caresses. Then she shook herself mentally. 'Snap out of it, stupid,' she muttered at her reflection in the bathroom mirror. 'You're behaving like a half-witted teenager. Those kisses mean nothing to him, so don't allow them to seep into your system. Don't allow them to become a drug so that you cry for more—and more.'

And with this sound advice swirling about in her mind she began to prepare the evening meal.

CHAPTER SIX

Lynn did not see Blair during the following week, and this, she assured herself, was a relief. Or was it? Relief, she realised, would have been more intense if she had been capable of getting him out of her mind—and if she had been able to forget those kisses in the kitchen.

But despite her efforts to do so she kept seeing his face with its regular features and tanned complexion, and she had only to close her eyes to recall the closeness of his athletic body pressing against her own. The aura of his masculinity seemed to wrap itself about her, and she found herself longing for the sound of his step on the front veranda, or his knock on the back door.

In fact he was so much in her thoughts that she even reached the stage of expecting to turn round and find herself confronted by him; but fortunately this did not happen, otherwise she might have revealed the turmoil raging within herself, as well as the depth of her yearning to see him.

At the same time she made valiant attempts to fasten her thoughts on her own work, but, although she spent hours at the typewriter, the stories made little progress while her memory seethed with the feel of his arms holding her against him, and the pressure of his lips on her own.

Nor did she see anything of Tony. Day after day she heard the school bus rumble past without stopping, and by the end of the week she was fighting a growing despondency. Blair had had a word with the bus driver, she decided. He'd arranged for the man to stop at

Marshlands and to forcibly evict one small disobedient lad whose desire was to go on to Frog Hollow.

Eventually she became aware that Max was observing her in his own quiet way, and therefore she was not surprised when the questions she guessed to be simmering in his mind were brought out into the open. Her problem then lay in knowing how to answer them.

'Are you becoming bored with this place?' he asked one afternoon.

She was startled by his abruptness. 'No, of course not, Grandy. What would put such a thought into your head?'

His eyes regarded her intently. 'I just wondered. You've been very silent for much of the week. Is anything wrong?'

She sent him a direct look. 'No. What could possibly be wrong?'

'The little boy hasn't been near us recently,' he observed.

'Hasn't he? I really hadn't noticed,' she responded carelessly. It was a lie and she knew it.

'Perhaps your thoughts are more with the big boy,' he remarked in a shrewd tone.

She laughed, brushing the suggestion aside. 'That's quite...*quite* ridiculous. You're my only big boy, Grandy.'

He ignored her banter by demanding abruptly, 'Have you had a quarrel with him? Has that fiery hair put sparks on your tongue?'

She avoided his eyes, then controlled a deep sigh that was about to escape her. 'You might as well know I'm not his most favourite person. He blames me for Tony's visits to this place. He thinks I'm encouraging disobedience in the boy and he...he even...' Words failed her as she recalled Blair's suspicions.

'Yes? He even what?' Max was watching her closely.

'He even fears I might be planning to take the boy to Delphine,' she admitted while trying to override the hurt caused by his distrust.

'I hope you wouldn't be stupid enough to make such an attempt,' Max growled, making no attempt to hide his irritation. 'There are passports and other travel formalities to be considered.'

'Don't worry, Grandy—no such idea entered my head. I'm not completely nutty, despite Blair's opinion of me. Besides, wouldn't I be in trouble with the law?'

'You can put a ring round the word trouble, and that's a fact.' He paused, looking at her reflectively. 'So, without the little boy to interrupt your afternoon, how much of your own work has been achieved this week?'

'Not very much,' she confessed. 'My mind keeps wandering. I need a few lessons in mental control.'

'You mean you need something to get the big boy out of your head,' he suggested drily. 'You can't fool me, my girl.'

'Will you *please* stop harbouring silly ideas, Grandy?' she flashed at him, then, fearing his acute perception, she added hastily, 'I think I'll give myself an exercise. I'll take a notebook out to the seat beneath the willow, and I'll observe. I'll write a few descriptions of the birds on the lake.'

'You'll find plenty there, especially if you throw stale bread on the water. The ducks will arrive at once, and the black swans will come quite close. Well, now—I'll be away to my club.'

A short time later she relaxed beside the water where the lake's feathered residents waited for more bread to the thrown. The silence of the still air was broken by the hum of bees in the hawthorn trees, and the warm sun on her back made her feel drowsy. Closing her eyes she sat listening, then opened them suddenly as the humming changed to the more intense drone of an aircraft.

Gazing into the distance, she saw a helicopter hovering like a giant bumble bee over the back hills of the Marshlands property. She then recalled that Grandy had said he'd been talking to Gary Palmer, who had told him the thistles on the hills were due to be sprayed.

As the dark spot moved against the sky her mind returned to her previous idea about city children staying in the country homestead. They would be there when the thistle-sprayer arrived, she now decided. The kindly pilot would take them up for a flight while becoming acquainted with the boundaries of the property.

Peering down from the helicopter the children would see a cave, which they would investigate as soon as the spraying work was finished. When they reached it they would discover articles that had been stolen during recent burglaries. The robbers would be caught, but exactly how this was to be achieved had yet to be solved in Lynn's mind.

A burst of enthusiasm sent her back to the cottage, where she settled herself at the typewriter. The afternoon sun shining through the alcove windows gave comfort to the room, and she no longer felt drowsy while tapping out the first draft of the story.

Her fingers flying over the keys, she became so engrossed she failed to hear Blair's knock on the front door, nor was she aware he had arrived until he tapped on the window while staring at her through the glass. The sight of him caused her heart to leap, and as she went to open the door she felt her cheeks become rosy.

They stared at each other in a long silence until she said, 'This is a surprise.'

'Pleasant, or otherwise?' he drawled, his eyes raking her face.

'That will depend upon the reason for your visit,' she returned, making an effort to control her inner excitement. 'If you're searching for Tony you'll not find him here.'

'I know where to find Tony,' he informed her. 'Sandra has taken him to town to buy new pyjamas. Apparently he's grown out of the old ones. Actually, it's you I've come to see.'

'Me?' Her breath quickened as she waited to hear more, and, looking at him wonderingly, she hoped her face did not betray the underlying gladness the sight of him gave her.

'Yes. Aren't you going to ask me in? Or are you too busy writing letters? I can guess to whom.'

'You're jumping to conclusions again,' she said without making further explanations, at the same time wondering why his presence made her feel like a jittery schoolgirl. 'Please come in.'

As he entered the living-room he said, 'Tomorrow I'm driving a few miles along the coast road to look at a pony for Tony. Would you like to come with me?'

She remained calm while endeavouring to conceal the surge of delight bubbling within her. 'That would be pleasant,' she said in the most casual tone she could produce. 'But you must realise I know nothing about horses.'

'You can leave the judgement of the purchase to me. However, if you'd rather not come——'

'Oh, yes, please. I'd like to come,' she assured him quickly.

'You'll not be too busy? When I looked in the window you appeared to be deep in thought. You hadn't heard my knock on the back door, nor on the front door, yet I felt sure you were here. I had no option but to look in the window, and there you were, surrounded by papers, and typing as though your life depended upon it.'

'It's just a small project of my own,' she admitted.

'You're making another attempt to write a story?'

'I suppose you could say so,' she admitted reluctantly. He looked interested. 'May I see it?'

'Certainly not.' Her words were emphatic.

'Very well, but better luck this time.' He brushed the subject aside by adding, 'I'll pick you up after lunch tomorrow.'

'Thank you. I'll be ready and waiting,' she promised.

There was no attempt to kiss her, Lynn noticed, watching him drive away. But it didn't matter. Tomorrow he'd be taking her out, which was something to look forward to. Nor was it easy to control the feeling of exhilaration that gripped her as she returned to the typewriter.

But despite her efforts to get back into the story her concentration had disappeared. Blair's face kept looming before her eyes, interrupting her train of thought until at last she gave an exclamation of impatience and went to the kitchen to prepare the evening meal. But even there she found herself pausing to gaze into space.

Next morning the sense of exhilaration was still with her, causing a light song to escape her lips as she cleared the breakfast table. And, although she tried to assure herself that this inner excitement had nothing to do with the prospect of going out with Blair, her basic honesty forced her to admit the truth.

Max looked at her with interest. 'You sound merry and bright this morning. I notice something has lit candles behind your eyes.'

She kept her back towards him as she said, 'I always feel good when I have a story running through my mind. It—it stimulates me.'

'In that case you'll be working all day?'

'No—only this morning. This afternoon I'll be going to look at a pony, with Blair.'

'Ah.' His tone held satisfaction.

'It's on the coast road. It's one he's considering for Tony.'

'And your valuable opinion is most necessary.' Max grinned.

'I know you're laughing at me, Grandy,' she protested. 'It's—it's just that I need to know about animals for—for my children's stories, you understand.'

He continued to grin. 'Oh, yes, I understand perfectly well. Of course you must learn about animals. Make sure you take a good look at the two-legged colt driving the car.'

'Why should I do that?' she queried loftily.

'Because he's a fine specimen. He's one that can be relied upon to run a straight race.' He shrugged himself into a jacket. 'Now then, I'll be away to my ewes. One is about to produce a late lamb.'

Lynn watched him stride away with Mick at his heels, then went to the typewriter where she remained until it was time to prepare lunch. But despite her efforts to concentrate the story refused to flow smoothly because anticipation caused constant pauses to glance at her watch, or to consider what she should wear. Nothing too dressy, she decided, otherwise it would look as if she hoped to impress him, and that was the last thing she had in mind. Or was it?

Eventually she decided upon an emerald leisure suit with pleated pants and a top that zipped up to a mandarin collar. Extra care was taken with her hair and her make-up, and when she emerged from the bedroom Max, who had returned for lunch, nodded his approval.

'You look fine,' he muttered. 'That green outfit makes your eyes look like traffic-lights, and your hair looks nice curling round that high collar. I dare say Blair will see these things for himself. He's not exactly blind.'

'I'd prefer him to keep his eyes on the road,' she retorted in a cool voice, then drew a sharp breath as she heard his steps on the front veranda.

He was casually dressed in fawn trousers that hugged his slim hips, while the oatmeal open-neck shirt revealed a triangle of crisp dark hairs on his chest. His eyes flicked over her as he entered the room, then he turned his attention to Max, telling the older man about the pony he intended to buy.

'It's a twelve-hand grey Welsh gelding,' he explained. 'Eight years old and very quiet. It should be suitable for Tony for several years.'

'Who owns it now?' Max queried.

'Bill Jordan who lives on Tamumu Road. His children have reached the stage of needing larger horses with more life in them,' Blair explained.

It was still early afternoon when they left, and as Lynn sat in the Peugeot she became aware of a feeling of serenity. She was also vitally conscious of the man sitting beside her, the subtle aroma of his aftershave indicating that care had been taken with his toilet before coming to take her out.

They drove eastward, through farming country, the green hills on their left being grazed by black Aberdeen Angus cattle. On their right were heavily fleeced sheep nibbling the lush flat pastures which stretched towards the river, which was concealed by a border of dense willows. Little was said as the road fell behind them, nor did conversation appear to be necessary.

All too soon—or so it seemed to Lynn—they turned in at an entrance where a metalled drive ran between fields towards a homestead. Blair stopped the car halfway along its length, then pointed to a grey pony grazing a short distance from the fence.

'There he is, waiting for a new owner to ride him.'

Lynn said, 'Tony will be delighted. Have you told him?'

'Definitely not. I must make sure the pony is suitable before allowing him to become excited about it. Quiet ponies for beginners are difficult to find.'

When they reached the house Bill Jordon emerged to greet Blair. He carried a tin which contained a few oats, and after being introduced to Lynn he went to the fence and banged the side of the tin with a stick while calling to the pony. The animal raised its head, regarded the tin, which received another bang, then trotted towards them.

Lynn watched with interest while Blair examined the pony by rubbing his hands over it, looking at its teeth and by walking it backwards and forwards. Its feet were checked, and at last he seemed to be satisfied. How much would he have to pay for it? she wondered, then guessed that the price would run into several hundred dollars at least. Yet he was willing to do this for Tony.

A short time later he wrote a cheque which he handed to Bill Jordon, and as they drove away he said with satisfaction, 'Bill will deliver Taffy tomorrow in his horse trailer.'

'Taffy? Of course—a Welsh pony.' Then she sent him an enquiring look. 'Shouldn't the pony have come home on trial before money changed hands?'

'I doubt that it's necessary in this case. I'm not unfamiliar with the animal, and I know Bill. He guarantees it to be free of vice and most suitable for Tony.'

'Oh. Well, it's nice to have confidence in people.'

'Yes, it is,' he returned drily.

A sudden despondency descended upon Lynn as she realised that Blair had much more confidence in Bill Jordon's word than he had in her own. In the midst of trying to shake it off she realised he had not turned for home after leaving the Jordon gateway, and therefore she straightened in her seat and asked quickly, 'Where are we going? Isn't home in the opposite direction?'

'I thought you'd never notice,' he said, grinning. 'Are you in a desperate hurry to return home, and to get on with that all-important project?'

'No, not really.' What did he have in mind? she wondered.

The answer came as though he'd read her thoughts. 'I've had a sudden urge to take a drive to the coast. I haven't walked on the sands since I've been home, and today seems to be appropriate.'

'Why would that be?' she asked carefully.

He thought for a while before he said, 'Perhaps buying the pony has made me feel light-hearted.'

'Perhaps that's as good a reason as any other for feeling happy,' she said, realising that his good spirits had nothing to do with the fact that they were going out together—though heaven alone knew what had put such an idea into her head. Nevertheless the beach lay at least twenty-four miles from Waipawa, so the outing was proving to be more than the promised short trip to look at a pony. A smile touched her lips as her own spirits lifted.

It caught his attention. 'Is it possible that you also feel a little light-hearted?'

'Light-headed would be a more apt term,' she admitted. 'This is an unexpected pleasure.' Then, fearing he could possibly take too much from that confession, she added hastily, 'You see, I've never been out to the coast in this district. Visits from home have always been too short to do so.'

He considered her reply in silence while staring ahead at the tarsealed road winding through the hilly country.

Contentment wrapped itself about her as she gazed at the high slopes where dark green pines and stately poplars held back slips of soil erosion, and eventually she asked, 'Are there hills all the way to the coast?'

'Yes, range after range of them, but apart from climbing over a few ridges the road finds its way along the valleys.'

They passed well-established country homes, most of them nestling within the shelter of plantations and approached by tree-lined drives. Sheep and cattle grazed the vivid green growth of spring pastures, shearing sheds stood surrounded by railed yards, and hay barns held the remains of winter feed.

'It all looks so peaceful,' Lynn was forced to comment.

He arched an eyebrow in her direction. 'Entirely different from your own environment at home, where there's the buzz of the community on all sides. I doubt that this tranquillity would suit you for long.'

She felt nettled. 'What makes you say that?'

'The fact that you're Delphine's friend. The old saying would prove itself to be true.'

She turned to stare at him. 'What old saying?'

'Birds of a feather flock together. Like Delphine, you'd become bored with the peace and quietness.'

'You're jumping to conclusions again.' She smiled, determined to not take offence. 'Frog Hollow is peaceful, and I'm not even remotely bored.'

He laughed. 'Give it time and you'll become fed up with the silence. At the moment it is just something that's different from home and all its hubbub of activity. In any case, Frog Hollow is close to town, but how would you feel about settling away out in the backblocks?'

'That would depend upon the man with whom I settled.' She sent him a sly peep of innocent enquiry. 'Tell me, Blair—are all men the same, or is it just that some disguise their male chauvinism more cleverly than others?'

'Are you suggesting there are no happy marriages?'

'No, of course not. My parents never hide the fact that they love each other. I think it keeps them feeling young.'

'My own parents are rather like that. Personally I consider it important for the right people to meet each other.'

Had he never met the right person? she wondered, taking unobtrusive glances at his handsome profile, and at his well-shaped hands resting on the steering-wheel. Not that the answer to that question really interested

her, of course. And then her thoughts were diverted as
they topped the summit of a long hill and were offered
a panoramic view of receding ridges which became lower
as they reached the coast. Beyond them lay the sea, a
vast expanse of blue stretching towards a distant horizon.

'That's the South Pacific Ocean,' he informed her.

'That much I happen to know,' she returned with a
laugh.

When they reached the coast he drove along a sea-
front road to where beach cottages nestled at the foot
of a line of sloping hills. Some of them were occupied,
although the majority appeared to be closed while
waiting for weekend residents.

A Norfolk-pine-sheltered turning bay at the end of the
road enabled him to point the car's bonnet towards
home, but instead of driving back at once he recalled
his earlier intention and switched off the motor. Then,
bending to unlace his shoes, he said, 'Let's go for a walk
along the sands.'

She followed suit by slipping off her own shoes and
the socks she wore beneath her leisure pants, then felt
suddenly carefree as she followed him over soft sand to
where a track ran beside the base of bare grey cliffs.

'This is called Muddy Point,' he informed her. 'This
track is just firm clay that has slid down from the cliffs.
It goes only a short distance.'

To their left a wide flat reef, cluttered with rocks and
large grey clay boulders, stretched towards the surf that
broke in a line of curling white foam. They wandered
across it, pausing at times to peer into pools glistening
between the rocks, or to pick up small iridescent shells
that glowed in a variety of pinks, blues and mauves.

On one slippery surface her foot slid, almost causing
her to overbalance, and it was only his swift grip on her
arm that saved her from falling. His hand then moved
to hold her own in a firm clasp, his touch sending tingles
through her nerves. She peeped at him, wondering if he

had sensed a similar effect, but his casual attitude gave no indication that holding her hand meant anything at all. Nor did he try to retain it when she released it gently.

Instead he gazed out to sea and said nonchalantly, 'If you swam far enough in a straight line you'd hit the south Chilean coast.'

'And very chilly you'd be,' she quipped back, glad of a diversion to help her feel normal. 'Don't let me stop you if you feel the urge to set off—but do watch out for sharks. I'll take the Peugeot home for you.'

'Do you think you could drive it?'

'I'd do my best not to hit anything.'

'I must let you take the wheel on some occasion.'

She gaped at him, scarcely able to believe her ears. 'You'd actually allow me to drive your—your precious Peugeot?'

'Why not? And what's so precious about it?'

His reply left her speechless, yet conscious of a growing suspicion. Was it her imagination that he was being especially nice to her? She felt sure it was not—therefore what did he have in mind? Was he trying to gain her confidence? Was that the entire reason she was being given this outing? The questions tumbled about in her thoughts, warning her to be on her guard. But against what?

And then her apprehensions were swept aside as she listened to his voice telling her of his more youthful days spent on this beach—of fishing trips in launches, and of moonlight picnics round bonfires built on the sands. Had she ever tasted foil-wrapped potatoes and sausages cooked in the hot embers? She hadn't? Then that omission in her education must be remedied.

She hardly noticed when they left the flat reef and reached the firm sand which made walking easier, and it was only when she turned round to look back that she realised how far they had wandered. The beach cottages were now hidden beyond Muddy Point, while the tips

of the Norfolk pines could be seen peeping above it.
'How far do you intend to walk?' she asked, forcing a
light tone into her voice.

'No further than this, because the tide's on its way
in.' He stood still, staring towards the upper reaches of
the beach, then added, 'We'll take a short rest on the
dry sand beside those coastal shrubs, then we'll head for
home.'

He took her hand again, then guided her across the
sands towards a position nicely protected from the cool
breeze that had now sprung up. The low growth of
coastal shrubs also sheltered them from the observation
of anyone who might walk along the sands, and as she
sat down she became aware of the isolation of the place.

For some unknown reason she began to feel tense,
waiting for she knew not what. However, within a short
time she realised her fears were groundless because
nothing happened. Blair merely lay back against the
sandy turf, his hands clasped behind his head while he
gazed at the sky.

'Old Max seems to be improving in health,' he remarked at last, his words coming as an anticlimax.

'Yes, thank goodness.'

'Your pleasant company and the good food placed
before him are beginning to show results.'

His words caused an inner glow which remained
hidden as she said, 'People living alone are apt to become
lazy about preparing meals for themselves.'

'So, how long do you intend staying with him?' The
question was put to her casually.

She thought for several minutes before answering. 'I
haven't decided,' she admitted at last.

'Your own special plans will not force you to leave?'
he drawled.

The mention of plans hit her ears with something of
a shock. The subject had come up before, she recalled,

but she merely smiled as she said, 'I'm not in any great hurry to rush away from Grandy.'

'Why do I get the feeling there's something you're not telling me?' he asked, turning on his side to look at her.

'Probably because your mind is good at building up suspicions. And may I point out that you've said very little about yourself? You know much more about me than I know about you,' she added, hoping to switch the conversation away from herself.

'Would you be interested?' he queried.

'Of course,' she exclaimed, hoping she didn't sound too eager.

He moved a few inches closer to her. 'Well, when I left boarding-school I came home expecting to begin work on Marshlands, but Dad had other ideas. He declared that a man who knew only his own small patch retained a small mind to match, therefore he sent me away to gain experience on other properties—but you already know that.'

Something stronger than herself forced her to say, 'There must have been an attractive daughter on at least one of those properties. Someone who could *ride*, and who wasn't a *city* type.'

'You're probing,' he teased accusingly. 'You're anxious to know whether or not I fell in love.'

'*Anxious?* Certainly not. Why should I be anxious?' she flared, furious with herself for having uttered the words, and aware that a flush had risen to her cheeks.

'Indeed, why should you care?' he drawled smoothly. 'However, I can assure you that marriage was the last thing on my mind because—like you—I had plans for overseas travel.'

His words amazed her. '*Like me?* Who says I have plans for overseas travel?'

'Sandra says she feels sure you're considering it,' he said, watching her through half-closed lids.

Indignation shook her. 'You've discussed me with *Sandra*?' she demanded angrily.

'There's no need to become ruffled,' he soothed. 'She was merely saying what she felt to be a fact.'

Lynn fought to control her irritation. 'I have *not* discussed overseas travel with Sandra. If she says so, she's lying. And for your information I haven't given it any thought at all.'

'Nevertheless you'll be off—sooner or later,' he persisted, watching her closely.

'Oh, perhaps at some time in the dim future,' she conceded, knowing that at present her books were keeping her too busy to think of travel—but there was no need to admit that fact.

'Possibly sooner than anyone realises,' he commented drily.

The words surprised her. 'What makes you so sure about that?'

'It's just a suspicion that keeps nagging at me.'

'*Suspicion?* Surely that word is too strong for something that can have little or no interest for you?'

'Perhaps I've given it more thought than you realise.' His eyes had become hooded, emphasising the shadows within their depths.

She gave a shaky laugh. 'I fail to see why any travel plans of mine could possibly interest you . . .' The words died on her lips as light dawned, causing her jaw to sag slightly. *Of course—travel plans to take Tony to his mother.* Her spirits plunged to zero, making her feel almost sick as she realised the depth of his distrust. Obviously, the plans hinted at by Grandy had been fanned into something more extensive by Sandra.

She took several deep breaths to control the angry words rising to her lips, and, while she longed to give vent to her feelings, she knew that to do so would cause a quarrel which would completely ruin the remainder of the afternoon. It was something she wished to avoid, therefore she switched back to the former topic of himself.

Forced brightness tinged her words as she said, 'Tell me more about your earlier years.'

He looked at her for several long moments then complied, perhaps because he too thought that a change of subject would be wiser.

Lynn's tension left her as she listened to his deep voice recounting incidents, and she also became convinced that Grandy was right in saying that Blair was a man of stability. A man to be relied upon. His loyalty to Stan was proof enough of that fact. Then, as she became even more comfortably relaxed, and despite her determination to avoid chatting about herself, she found small happenings with her own group of close friends slipping off her tongue.

Watching the animation on her face he queried casually. 'No doubt one of these city fellows was your...lover?'

She glared at him, her green eyes flashing with indignation. 'You've got a nerve to make such a suggestion. I've never had a lover—either in the true sense of the word, or in the way you mean.'

He frowned, then demanded sharply, 'The way I mean? What way would that be?'

'You're referring to a...a one-night stand—which is all you would be likely to offer,' she flung at him furiously, then, realising what she had said, a slow flush began to creep from her neck and up to her brow. She also became aware of how completely he had broken down her reserve. Well—not quite completely, she assured herself, because she had not yet admitted to her small success in the realm of children's books.

'I had no idea your opinion of me was so low,' he gritted. 'You make me sound like the proverbial tomcat.'

'Then hear this—I'm nobody's tabby,' she flashed at him.

His manner changed abruptly. 'I'm pleased about that,' he said in a low voice that had become husky, and, as he turned to face her, his arms slid round her body to draw her against him.

The action was so unexpected that she could only stare at him, her eyes widening with surprise, her instincts warning her to be wary.

Leaning over her he stared down into her face. 'Relax,' he advised. 'Get rid of that tension.'

She returned his gaze wordlessly, suspecting she was about to be kissed and wondering what she should do about it.

He guessed at her thoughts. 'Well—have you decided?'

'Decided about what?'

'Whether you'll scramble to your feet and race back to the beach cottages where you can yell for help, or be kissed like a sensible girl. Which is it to be?'

She continued to stare up into his face while turning the question over in her mind. 'Something tells me a sensible girl would flee for her life.'

'Are you always completely sensible?' The words were murmured in her ear while he nuzzled her ear-lobe.

She gave a shaky laugh. 'At the moment common sense seems to have been swept out to sea.'

'Good. I hope it stays there.' He lowered his head and found her lips with his own, brushing them backwards and forwards with a gentle seduction that sent her pulses racing.

She told herself that this was merely a momentary madness that must not be allowed to send her up into the clouds. She must keep control of her senses, and in a few moments the blood would cease to hammer in her temples.

His voice murmured against her mouth. 'Are your arms paralysed? Why aren't they round my neck?'

A sudden shyness engulfed her. 'Is that where you want them?'

'Do you have to be told?' The question came quietly.

Hesitantly she obeyed, her arms creeping up to enfold his shoulders until her fingers found the hair at the nape of his neck. As they entwined in it gently, she felt his quick intake of breath and the deepening of his kiss. Her lips parted, and, as his arms tightened about her, the urge to respond washed over her with the force of an ocean wave.

Vaguely, a voice whispered to watch her step, but it was hushed to oblivion by the flood of sensations surging through her body to lift her into the clouds. But as his hands kneaded their way down her spine to grip her buttocks and press her even closer, a small cry of protest escaped her. 'Please, Blair, no more...we must stop.'

'Please means more,' he teased. 'I can hear your heart beating. It seems to have gone wild.'

'It has not,' she denied breathlessly. 'That thump-thump is the sound of your own heart——'

'Then let me listen to make sure,' he laughed, making a rapid change of position which enabled him to lay his head against her breast. 'There, now—I told you so. I can hear every word it says.'

A tremor passed through her body, making it impossible to sound prosaic as she scoffed lightly, 'Non-sense——'

'It's being quite frank,' he assured her. 'It's crying out for us to make love.'

'Then it's telling lies because I have no inten-tion——'

'Not just at the moment, perhaps.'

'Not ever,' she exclaimed vehemently.

'You'd better believe the time will come,' he assured her while regarding her through eyes that were un-smiling, then a swift movement of his hand unzipped the front of her top, exposing the soft full roundness of her breast. His head bent quickly, his mouth finding the taut nipple.

She gasped at the unexpectedness of it, and despite the thrilling sensations that swept through her she struggled to pull up the zip. Pleasure weakened her indignation, but she managed to say, 'If you imagine that I'm your plaything to be picked up and then dropped—you can think again.'

'I'm not interested in playthings,' he told her seriously.

Her eyes held questions as she asked in a derisive tone, 'Then what are you interested in? An affair that gets nowhere?'

He turned and stared towards the sea. 'At the moment my main interest lies in the tide. If we don't move smartly we'll be unable to get past Muddy Point without a good soaking.' He stood up, then held out his hand to pull her to her feet, his arms again enfolding her and drawing her closely against his body.

Gazing at him mutely, she realised that his arousal had not subsided, and this became very evident as he kissed her once more, the fierceness of his mouth almost taking her breath away. But when he released her abruptly, then snatched at her hand to almost drag her along the upper reaches of the sand, she was unsure whether she was gripped by relief or disappointment.

CHAPTER SEVEN

THEY reached the firm track stretching towards Muddy Point with the water's edge lapping only a few feet away. Then, on the higher ground of the turning bay, they spent time in removing sand from their feet before putting on socks and shoes.

Blair grinned at Lynn. 'You've been saved by the tide.'

'Not entirely,' she informed him calmly. 'I still have a little will-power left.'

'You have? Something tells me it's been rocked into a state of shakiness since we've been here.'

She grasped at her dignity. 'That was only on the surface. Beneath it I can be quietly determined.'

'Determination can be broken down,' he reminded her, his arms again enfolding her while he kissed her gently before switching on the ignition.

Little was said as they drove past the beach cottages and parked caravans awaiting their weekend occupants, and as she gazed across the bay towards a distant hilly point Lynn tried to ignore the sensation of dreamy pleasure that persisted in wrapping itself about her. She knew its cause emanated from being with the man sitting beside her, and she was also aware that her feelings towards Blair Marshall had taken on a subtle change. Changed, or advanced? she asked herself.

And if it had not been for the tide, what price would her own will-power have been worth? Closing her eyes, she relived the moments of lying in his arms, his lips on her own, his head against her breast. The memory of her own longing sent a warm flush to her cheeks, a flush that deepened as she recalled his mouth on her nipple, and his words, 'The time will come.'

And then the sound of his deep voice came to her ears, causing her eyes to fly open. 'Have you gone to sleep?'

'No, I...I was just resting my eyes——'

'Don't you mean you were just...remembering?' The question came softly as he sent her a rapid glance.

The wide eyes she turned upon him were filled with their own questions, yet she was unable to voice them aloud. What did *he* feel about those moments of closeness? Had he already shrugged them off? If so she had better steel herself to do likewise. She'd be a fool to allow a few kisses to go to her head.

Again he spoke softly, his voice now teasing. 'You *were* remembering. It's useless to deny it.'

She spent another few moments in silence then admitted shyly, 'It's left me feeling slightly shaken.'

'Only slightly?' he asked quietly.

She looked away, not willing to reveal just how shaken she had been, and in fact still felt. Then, suddenly irritated by the way in which her emotions were getting out of hand, she sent him a glance that was full of reproach. 'At least you appear to be completely unaffected—but no doubt you're accustomed to such encounters.'

An exclamation of impatience escaped him. 'You appear to be tossing the ball back into my court. Is this because you refuse to let me know anything at all about your feelings?'

'My feelings are my own private business,' she hedged.

'And kept locked away in an icebox,' he retorted. 'Are you always so hard to reach? Is it impossible to draw close enough to learn of your hopes and plans for the future?'

She laughed, refusing to be drawn. 'Plans? I've no intention of ruining these moments by returning to *that* particular subject.'

'You're enjoying them?' he queried softly, stretching a hand to clasp her own which rested in her lap.

She nodded without speaking, thrilling to the pressure of his fingers before they returned to the wheel. After that she noticed that he appeared to be in no hurry to reach home. Instead he drove at a leisurely pace, giving them both time to observe the purple shadows gathering between the folds of the hills, and to watch the sky becoming streaked with reds and golds above the distant Ruahine ranges.

It was dusk by the time they reached Frog Hollow. The cottage was dark and silent, the empty space in the garage indicating that Max had not yet returned from his afternoon session at the club. However the surrounding area was anything but silent because the frogs had started their evening chorus.

Blair said, 'I'll come inside and check the cottage. One never knows who could be lurking behind a door or under a bed.'

His thoughtfulness pleased her. 'Thank you. I'm afraid Grandy never bothers to lock doors. He declares that even a blind burglar could see there's little of real value in this old place.'

He took her hand as they went towards the cottage, and she felt a tingling thrill from the pressure of his fingers. They entered the living-room where he kissed her briefly, then she knelt to put a match to the open fire while he switched on the lights. She then went to the kitchen to turn on the oven which would heat the previously prepared casserole.

She had not felt nervous about entering the dark cottage, but his action had delayed his departure, and she knew she didn't want him to leave. She sighed, thinking it would have been nice to have spent the evening together, but no suggestion to do so had been made. Then, looking at the casserole, impulse made her call to him from the kitchen, 'Would you like to join us for evening meal?'

There was no reply, and, puzzled by his silence, she returned to the living-room to find it empty. However, the glow of her bedroom light revealed him to be in the room with one of her books in his hand.

He turned slowly as she entered, his tight mouth and slightly narrowed eyes making no secret of his anger as he rasped, 'There appears to be more of interest on the table than behind the door or under the bed.'

'Oh?' She put on a show of nonchalance.

His tone held a ring of accusation. 'You're not struggling to write stories. These books prove you to be a published author of children's literature.'

'Yes, well . . . so what?'

'Why didn't you tell me?' The question came coldly.

'I don't usually shout it from the roof-tops.'

'You could have told me. The subject did come up.'

'And you were rather amused. You were somewhat patronising, if I remember correctly,' she reminded him in a dry tone.

'I was merely encouraging you to keep trying—and all the time you'd actually reached this stage,' he gritted, almost slamming the book on the table. 'It must have given you a good laugh.'

She felt guilty. 'Of course it didn't. And I would have told you—sooner or later.'

He went on, his anger unabated, 'This is exactly what I mean when I say I can't reach you. You hold out on me.'

'Why should you want to reach me?' She held her breath, waiting for his answer.

'So that I can trust you,' he snapped.

The words were hurtful, but she raised her chin bravely. 'There's no reason for you to distrust me.'

'I'm beginning to wonder about that.' His dark grey eyes held a bleak glint as his brows drew together and his jaw tightened. Then his tone became frigid. 'If you've been so secretive about this project, it makes me wonder what else you have in mind.'

She gave a derisive laugh as she said scathingly, 'Such as a plan to take Tony to England without a passport?'

His voice became hard. 'For your information, the boy already has a passport. The only trouble is, we can't find it.' He looked at her searchingly with eyes that were like pebbles. 'I told you his mother tried to take him with her when she left. His passport was arranged for then, but now it appears to have disappeared.'

She stared at him, her eyes wide with incredulity as his words sank into her brain, then a small gasp escaped her as she demanded, 'Are you suggesting that in some mysterious way this missing passport went hoppity-hop all the way to Frog Hollow?' The idea was so ludicrous it caused a ringing laugh to escape her.

He remained serious, then rasped pointedly, 'You were in the boy's room. His passport—according to Sandra— was in a folder with his birth certificate. She says the folder was lying in a top drawer.'

Icy fingers began to make themselves felt within her chest, then her voice shook as she said, 'You're accusing me of *stealing* it? Don't you know that Maisie was with me the entire time? How could I search drawers in her presence?'

'Sandra says that Maisie probably left you alone for a few minutes after she herself went downstairs to prepare Tony's evening meal. But I'll admit that Maisie denies this.'

'You sound as if you're reluctant to believe her. Is this because you prefer to believe Sandra?' Lynn's voice held dismay.

His expression became bleak. 'Sandra says that Maisie has either forgotten she left you in the room, or won't admit it. I'm afraid they've had a real quarrel about it.'

Lynn's fury burst forth as she almost shrieked, '*Sandra says—Sandra says*—how *dare* she imply that I'm a thief—and how dare you listen to her?'

'Calm down,' he advised. 'There's no need to burst into flames. Nor can you blame me for wondering what it all adds up to.'

'*All what* adds up to?' Her voice was still raised.

'Your friendship with Delphine, and towards the boy—and now there's the matter of his missing pass-port——'

'About which I know nothing. Do you understand? *Nothing.*' She swung round and left him, returning to the living-room where she threw a log of wood on the fire. For several moments she stood watching the sparks rise up the chimney, then she sank into a chair while a cloak of depression began to wrap itself about her. Well, at least she knew where she rated in his opinion. Somewhere near the bottom of the popularity poll.

He followed her into the room then stood regarding her huddled form in moody silence until he said, 'You look as though you're sitting under a dark cloud. May I pour you a drink?'

'No, thank you. It would choke me. But help yourself.'

'Thank you.' He went to the cabinet, then turned to look at her. 'Are you sure you won't have a sherry? It might help you to think a little more clearly.'

She blinked back the tears, then dabbed at her eyes while his back was turned towards her. 'My thinking is quite clear—thank you very much for suggesting it *isn't*. I can see the whole situation very clearly without the aid of sherry. I can see exactly why you took me for that drive this afternoon.' Her tone had become bitter.

'You're sure about that?'

'It's more than obvious. Your aim was to gain my confidence. It was part of a softening-up process, and during it you hoped I'd betray whatever plan I had in mind. Only there isn't a plan. As for the rest of the afternoon...' She fell silent as words failed her, while making an effort to control tears.

'You mean when we lay so close together?' he queried delicately.

'Please, don't remind me—I'd rather forget it.'

'Is that something else you're sure about?'

'Absolutely positive. The memory gives me a pain because now I know it was all so... so insincere. I'm sorry I caused you to put on such an act to learn of something that wasn't there.'

He frowned. 'What do you mean?'

'Well, I should have told you about my books earlier. I should have explained they were published only through Delphine's help, so that when she asked me to make a report to her about Tony I felt obliged to do so. I felt I owed it to her. But let me assure you that the thought of taking him to her never entered my head, nor has she ever asked me to do so. That's all there is to the situation—nothing more, nothing less.'

He sipped his drink thoughtfully until at last he said, 'Very well—I'll make an effort to believe you.'

'Don't strain yourself,' she lashed at him wrathfully.

He remained calm. 'I hope I haven't upset you too much.'

She spoke coldly. 'I'm not accustomed to people doubting my integrity to such an extent.'

He stared into his glass. 'What can I say or do to put matters right? I dislike this antagonism between us.'

She ignored his plea for peace. 'You can finish your drink and get out of my sight.' Acute misery dragged the words from her.

'Does that mean you don't want to see me again—ever?'

'You've read the signs correctly.'

'Very well.' He drained his glass, put it on the table then went to the door. Opening it, he paused to turn and look at her, his voice remaining cool as he said, 'Goodnight, Lynn.'

'*Goodbye*, Blair.' She kept her gaze fixed on the flames, not daring to let him see the unhappiness she feared might be reflected within the depths of her eyes.

His step on the veranda echoed faintly, and moments later the sound of the Peugeot backing out of the drive was barely discernible. As it faded she hurried to the bathroom where cold water was splashed on her eyes before Grandy could see traces of tears.

Fortunately, Max was later than usual in arriving home, and when he eventually walked in the door his mind appeared to be full of a controversy that had taken place at the club—too full of it in fact to notice Lynn's subdued state of mind.

She listened patiently while he expounded upon the argument that had taken place, and at last she was able to escape to bed, where she reviewed her own controversy with Blair. As she did so her eyes filled with tears which trickled unheeded into the pillow.

She'd been a fool, she decided. She should have told him about her books ages ago, and then this situation might not have arisen. Further, she'd reacted too strongly to his suspicions concerning her intentions towards Tony. Why couldn't she have remained calm instead of allowing her anger to bubble and boil out of control?

As for those kisses at the beach—it was now obvious they had meant less than nothing to him, therefore the sooner she wiped them from her memory the better. After all, she was here to take care of Grandy, and to compile a new set of children's stories. She was *not* here to become emotionally involved with a devastating man like Blair Marshall who—if she was not careful—would only lead her into a vale of tears from which she would never emerge.

So why was she weeping now? Why was she shedding tears over a man who would waft her up into clouds of delight, then drop her to the depths of depression in his efforts to learn of any kidnapping plans she might have?

She thumped the pillow and turned over in bed, but despite her efforts to sleep she lay wide-eyed in the darkness. Outside the silence was broken by the occasional bleat of a sheep, while the croaking of frogs came softly from the large water-filled hollow.

'Work is what I need,' she muttered aloud, then sat up to switch on the bedside light. 'Now is the time for a little progress on that story about the cave in the hills.'

She reached for a pad and pen, intending to scribble whatever came into her head, but even as she stared at the blank page the outline of dark brown hair and brows swam into her vision. She saw the grey eyes glinting at her coldly, and the mobile mouth that had kissed her during the afternoon. Even the feel of his hands seemed to caress her body, the memory causing her nerves to quiver.

And then she recalled his deep voice uttering suspicions that she could have stolen Tony's passport with the intention of taking the boy to his mother. Sandra says this, Sandra says that . . . All his suspicions, she realised, had been planted and then fanned into flame by Sandra. OK, so let him question her sanity, but how dared he doubt her integrity?

Anger shook her as she flung down the pad and reached for a book, but the words made little sense. The story revolved round an encounter, but even this was something that struck at her troubled state of mind because her association with Blair was proving to be exactly that. Nothing more and nothing less than a brief encounter at Frog Hollow.

Eventually it was sheer weariness that sent her to sleep, although it was a night of restless slumber filled with dreams that caused her to toss and turn. When she woke next morning she felt heavy-eyed, nor did a yawn that escaped her during breakfast miss the sharp eyes of her grandfather.

'You slept badly?' he asked.

'Yes. I kept waking after silly dreams,' she admitted.

He was mildly interested. 'Anything prophetic?'

'Prophetic? No. Like most dreams they were utterly stupid. I seemed to be chasing Tony's grey pony along the beach.'

His eyes twinkled. 'Are you sure it wasn't a certain dark colt with grey eyes? Did you catch him?'

Weariness made her snap crossly, 'I know what you're getting at, Grandy, but you can forget it. I doubt that I'll be seeing him again—*ever*—so you can keep your hints to yourself.'

Max's shaggy grey brows drew together while his eyes became piercing. 'Had a quarrel, huh?'

'You can say *that* again,' she retorted as anger loosened her tongue. 'Would you believe he had the utter *temerity*, the colossal *nerve* to suggest I had plans to whip Tony off to his mother in England? Have you ever heard of anything more ridiculous?'

Max continued to frown. 'You can't blame him for wondering why you encourage the boy to come here, and you are friendly with his mother,' he reminded her by way of further explanation for Blair's suspicions.

Her voice rose as her anger became more intense. 'But not so friendly that I'd break the law by illegally removing him from the custody of his father. Good grief—I'd have to be out of my mind. How *dare* Blair imagine I'd be so *stupid*? It infuriates me to realise he looks upon me as a complete idiot.'

'Perhaps he's had previous experience with redheads,' Max remarked drily. 'It's possible he realises they can be impulsive and that there's no knowing what rash ideas will take hold of them. You must remember he feels responsible for the boy.'

Her eyes filled with reproach. 'Whose side are you on, Grandy?'

'Yours, of course, but in all fairness I'm trying to see Blair's side as well,' Max said quietly.

'You men sure stick together.' Her words held bitterness.

He went on unperturbed. 'Nor do I wish to see an end to your association with him. He's not like some of those long-haired layabouts you'll find in the city.'

She became indignant. 'I do not associate with long-haired layabouts. My friends are all young professionals with careers ahead of them.'

'Are they, indeed? Well, don't you worry, lass. Blair will be back—just like the black swan out on that water.'

Her green eyes flashed as she stood up and began to clear away the breakfast dishes. 'Get this straight, Grandy. I am not worrying about whether or not Blair will come back.'

'No? Well, that's just splendid,' he retorted drily. 'So what are you plans for today? More letter-writing to that woman in England, I suppose?'

'Certainly not. Delphine has had sufficient information to keep her satisfied for a while. Today I shall concentrate on the cave in the hills story. I've thought of a few mysterious happenings that will help me to stretch it to book length.'

'It sounds as if you'll be glued to your typewriter all day, and tomorrow, and the next day.'

'That's my intention exactly, Grandy. It's high time I got down to real work instead of frittering away hours at places like Pourerere Beach.' The words died on her lips as she recalled those moments on the upper sands when he had dragged her against him, his mouth crushing down upon her own. The memory caused pain to twist at her heart, her eyes becoming so blurred that she was unable to see beyond the kitchen window.

Hastily she became busy at the sink of hot water, lifting the dishes from it and placing them in a draining-rack where they dried within a short time. From the corner of her eye she saw her grandfather go outside to gather kindling for the living-room fire, and as he carried it past her she heard him mutter something about pride being the death of many a fine romance.

She longed to point out that romance between Blair and herself hadn't even begun, but knew her grandfather would not be convinced. Nor would he understand—no matter how hard she tried to explain—that their association had barely advanced beyond the stage of being an encounter.

He would look at her searchingly, and, with his uncompromising frankness, he would demand to know if Blair had kissed her. And she knew she'd be unable to lie to him. The annoying flush that rose to her cheeks so easily would give her away at once. It would tell him all he needed to know.

It was a relief to see him walk up the hill towards his sheep before more questions could be asked. Mick trotted obediently at his heels, and the moment they were out of sight Lynn went to the typewriter where she worked on *Cave in the Hills*. But despite her efforts to concentrate she found her ears constantly stretched for the sound of a tread on the front veranda, or a knock on the back door.

But it did not come. Nor was it likely to come, she realised sadly. Blair had said goodnight in a polite manner. But she had returned her goodbye with force. And as she thought of it now she knew that the statement had had a final ring to it. It was as if she'd closed a door that should have been left open—or at least ajar—and already she was beginning to regret it. '*Goodbye,*

Blair'—the words seemed to haunt her by flinging themselves back in her face.

Straightening her back from a slumped position that betrayed her dejection, she left the typewriter and went out to the front veranda. Fresh air was what she required, she told herself while taking in deep gulps of the crisp atmosphere in an effort to clear her mind of all its disturbing thoughts.

Her eyes turned towards the lake where she could see teal and grey duck feeding as they waddled along the edge. And then her attention was caught by the sight of a black swan gliding above the zigzag, its long neck and wings outstretched, its feet ready to paddle the moment it splashed down on the water.

Watching its return caused her spirits to rise, while her grandfather's words flashed into her mind. Could she take it as an omen that Blair—like the black swan—would also return? Perhaps this evening? But there was no sign of him that evening—nor during the days that followed.

It was strange how the passing of time softened one's anger, Lynn thought a week later. She had made good progress with the cave story, mainly because she had used will-power to push all disturbing thoughts from her mind, and she had shared the intrigue and excitement of her young characters. She had also been thankful that Max had been able to supply the necessary helicopter details.

By the end of ten days Blair had still not been near the place, and while she refused to allow herself to think about him there were times when memory became overpowering. During those moments she found herself gazing into space while recalling the intensity of his lips on her own, or the strength of his arms holding her close to his body. Had it all been little more than a sham on his part?

As for Tony, she decided he must surely be riding Taffy each day, and it needed little imagination to see the joy on his face when given his first sight of the grey Welsh pony. Dobbin in the nursery would now be neglected in favour of the real thing.

And then the afternoon came when a knock on the back door announced the boy's arrival, his face beaming as he said, 'Hi, Lynn. I've gotta pony, a *real* one. I want you to come and see Taffy. He's at the top of the zigzag.'

'You're out riding alone?' Lynn asked, feeling apprehensive.

'No. Sandra's up there too. She wouldn't let me ride down the zigzag. She said it's too steep, but some day I'll do it.' His hazel eyes glistened at the thought.

Lynn was surprised. 'Sandra allowed you to come and fetch me?'

He grinned at her. 'She doesn't know I've come. She didn't see me run down the zigzag because she was talking to Gary. She talks to him every time we go riding.'

Lynn laughed. 'Does she, indeed?'

Tony nodded. 'He's mending the fence near the top of the zigzag so I suppose that's why we came this way. I tethered Taffy a short distance from them and came to find you. Please come and see my pony,' he pleaded.

She looked at him doubtfully, knowing that Sandra would not welcome her arrival, then she shrugged off the knowledge. 'Very well—why not?' she said.

She followed the boy round the end of the lake, Tony racing ahead until they came to the zigzag which they climbed together. A short distance from the top Sandra stood talking to a man who was replacing battens in the fence.

Sandra appeared to be laughing happily but swung round as they approached. She glared at Lynn, then snapped at Tony, 'Didn't I tell you not to go down that zigzag?'

Lynn ignored her anger as she said calmly, 'He came to fetch me to see his pony. Is that such a crime?'

'Blair doesn't want him to associate with you,' Sandra snapped viciously. 'I'm to see he doesn't go near you. You're considered to be dangerous.'

The man working at the fence laughed as he regarded Lynn with interest. 'She doesn't look particularly dangerous to me,' he drawled to Sandra. 'Why don't you introduce us and let me judge for myself?' Then, as Sandra retained a sulky silence, he spoke to Lynn. 'I'm Gary Palmer.'

Lynn smiled at him. 'Yes, I know. Blair told me you're holding the fort for Stan while he's on holiday. I'm Lynnette Nichols. Actually, I've already seen the pony. Blair took me with him when he went to purchase Taffy. He seems to be very quiet.'

'Of course he's quiet—otherwise he wouldn't have been bought,' Sandra said scathingly. 'And he's proving to be the answer to our problem with Tony.'

Gary echoed his disbelief. 'Tony's a problem? In what way?'

Sandra explained acidly, 'Instead of getting off the school bus at the *right* place, he'd formed the habit of getting off at the *wrong* place. *She* encouraged him, of course.'

'Do you think he needed much encouragement?' Gary grinned.

The query served as a fan to Sandra's anger, goading her to lash at Lynn. 'Naturally, you had a reason for doing so—a devious plan in mind. But that plan has now been nipped in the bud by Blair's brilliant idea of purchasing the pony.'

Gary sounded intrigued. 'Tell me more. What sort of devious plan could she have?'

Lynn found difficulty in controlling her temper. Her cheeks burned and her eyes flashed green sparks as she glared at Sandra. 'You've got a nerve to suggest I have a devious plan,' she hissed. 'What gives you such a stupid idea?'

Sandra regarded her coldly. 'It was the fact that I couldn't find Tony's passport. I heard Blair tell Maisie that you're friendly with his mother. It made me wonder if you had plans to take him to her—and that made me realise we should keep an eye on his passport. But when I tried to find it, it was missing. And, what's more, it is still missing.'

'You needn't look at me,' Lynn informed her coldly. 'I've never set eyes on it.'

Sandra continued to glare at her accusingly. 'Blair knows it is still missing. Naturally, I've warned him about your intentions.'

Gary glanced at Tony, who stood listening to the exchange between Sandra and Lynn. He patted the boy's head and said, 'Come along, young fellow—I'll give you a leg up. It's time Sandra continued with your riding lessons.'

Sandra swung round to stare at him. 'That sounds as if I'm being dismissed,' she said resentfully.

He ran a hand through his fair hair while sending her a look of impatience. 'Take it any way you like. The point is that I'm supposed to be hammering in staples and I'd like to get on with the job, so if you'll excuse me...'

Sandra's chin rose. 'Very well—I'll see you again when the place isn't so *crowded*.' The last words were accompanied by a baleful glare at Lynn, then she placed a foot in the stirrup and swung herself into the saddle of her own mount.

Lynn watched until the two horses and their riders had disappeared beyond the trees surrounding the hay barn, then she turned to leave, bidding Gary goodbye.

He spoke casually. 'There's no need for you to dash away in a hurry. I can talk while I work.'

'I'm sure you can—but I have things to do at home.'
She left him and went towards the zigzag.

'See you around,' he called after her. 'I'll be on this
job again tomorrow,' he added hopefully.

'That'll be nice for you,' she flung over her shoulder,
then caught her breath as she saw Blair leave the shelter
of the hay barn and canter along the track towards the
boundary fence.

Her heart leapt when she saw him pause only briefly
to speak to Gary and then ride towards herself. Did he
suspect her of wasting Gary's time with idle chatter—
or was he about to accuse her of trespassing? 'Just you
keep off my property,' he'd once snarled at her.

And while a rebellious streak that was part of her
nature urged her to remain and face him with defiance,
another section of her mind prompted her to hasten with
all speed down the zigzag. It was the latter reasoning to
which she listened.

CHAPTER EIGHT

BLAIR shouted to her from the top of the zigzag. 'Hi, Lynn! What's the hurry? I want to talk to you...'

She ignored his words and almost raced down the last part of the track towards the fence. As she climbed over it she looked up and realised he had tethered his horse and was now following her, bounding down the track with the swiftness of an antelope. As she fled round the end of the lake she heard the creak of wires, then knew she was no match for the speed of his long legs.

He caught her at the cottage doorway, his arms snatching her to him while she gasped against his chest, too breathless to struggle from his grip that had the strength of iron bands.

'Why are you running away like a scared rabbit?' he demanded crossly, his breath also coming heavily.

'Wh—what do you want?'

'Just to talk to you. Is that so impossible?'

'Not really, I suppose. You'd better come inside and then you'll be able to blow my head off for trespassing on your property. I haven't forgotten your previous warning.'

He gave a snort of amusement. 'You haven't, huh?'

'No. Actually, I was there only because Tony wanted me to see Taffy. I couldn't disappoint him by refusing to go.'

'I'm aware of that fact. I spoke to Sandra as they were passing the hay barn. She told me he'd disobeyed orders and had run down to Frog Hollow to fetch you while she'd been talking to Gary. I also realise the daily rides take them to wherever Gary happens to be working.' He paused then asked, 'I presume Max is at his club?'

'Yes. He's fortunate to be able to go to a place where he can enjoy male company.' Speaking of her grandfather enabled her to feel more normal. It helped to subdue the flutter of excitement that made her fingers tremble as she put a match to the open fire in the livingroom.

As she knelt before it, her mind reached back to the last time they had been together in this room. It was less than a fortnight ago, yet it seemed as if an age had passed, and suddenly she realised how nice it was to see him there. She also realised how very much she had missed him.

She was aware that he now observed every movement she made, and the knowledge filled her with a selfconscious nervousness. Her hand became unsteady as she placed thicker lengths of wood on the flames, and when one log rolled on to the hearth he was beside her in an instant, adjusting the building of the fire.

Together they knelt on the hearthrug, the brush of his arm against her own sending a tremor through her nerves. The rising flames threw a glow of warmth to their faces, and suddenly the room became filled with an aura of intimacy which Lynn found to be most disconcerting.

In an effort to keep matters on an even keel she stood up abruptly and moved away from him. 'You said you wanted to talk to me,' she reminded him, trying to make her voice sound nonchalant.

He rose to his feet, thrust his hands into his pockets and stood with his back to the fire. His words came casually. 'Maisie thinks it is time you and Max came to have dinner with us.'

She hid her surprise. 'This is an invitation?'

'Of course. What else could it be?'

'From Maisie?' The question came hesitantly.

'She's my hostess, you know. At least there are times when she acts as my hostess. And she admits she has taken a liking to you. I believe she would like to know you better.'

'You're saying she doesn't look upon me as a *thief*?' she asked pointedly. 'Well, that's very sweet of her. To be honest I rather liked her too.' She thought for several moments then sent him a direct look as she queried, 'Therefore this invitation is from Maisie? It is not from yourself.'

He contemplated her in silence before he said, 'If I admit the invitation is from me I dare say you'll turn it down flat. I recall that you said "goodbye" with some force, so no doubt I'll have words to the effect of never darkening your door again flung at me.'

'No. I've got over that particular upset, although I'll confess I was very hurt at the time.'

'I didn't mean to hurt you.'

'In that case I hope I never see you in action when you *do* mean to hurt me.' The words were spoken seriously.

'Such a time will never come,' he assured her quietly.

She sent him a bleak look, wondering why she felt doubtful, then a bitter laugh escaped her as she said, 'In the meantime I'm to take the accusations of stealing a passport and kidnapping a child in my stride? I'm to brush them aside as being of no importance to my integrity? Personally, I can't understand how you could believe it of me, especially after...' She fell silent as words failed her.

His voice came crisply. 'I don't think it of you. At least, not any longer. Clear thinking soon told me the whole idea was too preposterous for words. Nor could I see what you would have to gain by the action.'

'Then why make such an accusation?' she demanded fiercely. 'Especially after we'd been so...so close.' This time the final words were dragged from her.

He took a deep breath that was almost a sigh of resignation as he said, 'I can only say the suggestion had been planted in my mind, and I had difficulty in ridding myself of it.'

'Planted by Sandra,' Lynn said, her lip curling with disdain.

'I suppose she felt obliged to tell me of her fears,' he excused. 'And, believe me, I was desperate to hear your denials and the assurance that you were harbouring no such ideas.'

She looked at him reproachfully, her heart twisting as she remembered the quarrel that evening when they had returned from the beach.

Almost reading her thoughts, he said, 'Perhaps I was tactless in quoting Sandra. I should have been more diplomatic.'

'More *trusting* is a better word,' she told him bitterly. 'The fact that you don't trust me really gets under my skin. It bugs me until I could *scream* every time I think of it——'

His hands grabbed her shoulders, giving her a definite shake while he broke in impatiently, 'So, have a good scream and get it off your chest. And then it might be possible for you to see *my* side of the situation. Despite our closeness at the beach I kept wondering if there were plans simmering in your mind. Were you scheming to abduct the boy—for whom I'm responsible—even while your arms were about my neck?'

'No—no—of course *I was not*,' she almost shrieked at him, wrenching herself angrily from his grip. 'My oath—you must think I'm *dumb*. Do you honestly believe I'm so dim-witted I can't see that Tony is better off at Marshlands than in London?'

'I would have thought it was more than obvious to anyone.'

She rushed on, 'And I haven't forgotten that it was Delphine who left Tony—therefore, if she wishes to see him let her return to New Zealand to do so. She can fly from London to Auckland, and then from Auckland to Napier, which is only forty miles away from here. I'm sure someone would drive Tony to Napier to see her.'

'Certainly not,' he snapped. 'She can come the full distance.'

'Are you always such a hard man?'

'Can't you understand I'm thinking of the boy? My concern is entirely with him. What happens when he has to leave her and come home to Marshlands?'

What, indeed? she wondered dolefully to herself, then tried to hide her anxiety as she asked, 'Do you still think it's a crime for me to write and tell her about him?'

'No. I think I can see reason on that point,' he conceded, then surprised her by asking, 'Do you feel this little chat has cleared the air—or has it made matters worse between us?'

'Could they be worse?' she asked with forced sweetness.

'Only by the continuation of misunderstanding—which is something I'd like to avoid.'

His last words caused her spirits to rise. Did he actually care whether matters between them were better or worse? The thought that perhaps he did brought a smile to her face as she admitted, 'I feel things are better. It's as if a black cloud has lifted.'

He regarded her intently. 'You felt it too, that black cloud? You've been depressed?'

She nodded. 'Our quarrel made me unhappy. I hate quarrels.'

'So do I. Shall we start afresh with a promise of no more tiffs?'

'Yes, please...that would be lovely.' She looked at him expectantly. Quarrels were usually made up with a kiss, she thought, waiting for his embrace, but he made no move to take her in his arms.

Instead he remained standing before the fireplace where the logs still crackled brightly, and, without looking at her, he said, 'About coming to dinner—would tomorrow evening be suitable?'

'Only for me, but not for Grandy,' she told him. 'It's his Rotary Club meeting where an evening meal is served.'

'In that case we'll rescue you from eating alone. Shall I call for you at six o'clock?'

'There's no need. I have my own transport, but thank you for the thought,' she replied with dignity while fighting the inner frustration his lack of affection had caused.

'Nevertheless I shall call for you, Miss Independence. But now I must go back to see how far Gary has progressed with renewing those fence battens. He's a good worker, and when Stan returns Gary will be retained as his assistant. I'm sure Sandra will be more than delighted.' He grinned.

'She'll be ecstatic,' Lynn agreed drily, realising that Blair's thoughts were more with other people than with herself.

He left a few minutes later, still without touching her, and leaving her even more conscious of disappointment. And as she stood at the back door watching him stride round the end of the lake the disappointment changed to a sense of loss.

Despite the mending of the quarrel between them he appeared to have become withdrawn from her, and she realised there would be no more kisses or affectionate embraces. Tomorrow night she need expect nothing more than a meal and friendship. Very well—so be it. At least she knew where she stood with him. Precisely nowhere.

The knowledge nagged painfully, and that night she lay in the darkness of her bedroom with more tears trickling into her pillow. She told herself she was being a fool and that there was nothing to weep about, but somehow she was unable to convince herself. They'd made friends, hadn't they? All was now well between them, wasn't it? Then why this deep depression? Why had the black cloud returned?

Honesty forced her to admit that its cause lay in the fact that Blair had failed to take her in his arms, and suddenly she knew that that was where she longed to be. Did this mean she was merely craving male affection—or did it mean she was falling in love with him?

When Lynn told her grandfather she would be having dinner at Marshlands, Max made no effort to hide his satisfaction. He watched her put rollers in her newly washed hair, then demanded to be shown the dress she intended to wear.

The request made her laugh. 'Don't fuss, Grandy— it's not a large dinner party,' she assured him. 'It's only little me. Blair is being kind for some strange reason.' Of this she felt sure.

'Hmm. Perhaps.' Max did not sound convinced, but later he expressed his approval of her appearance. 'There's no need to say you look quite stunning, I suppose.'

She felt pleased, because he was not a man from whom compliments came readily. 'Thank you, Grandy. Mind you're not late for Rotary.'

She surveyed herself in the long mirror attached to the wardrobe door, then felt a rush of gratitude towards the saleswoman who had talked her into purchasing the expensive dress and matching jacket. Fashioned in fine wool and cut on modern lines, its deep creamy colour sent lights into her hair. The low round neck was decorated by an inch-wide shell-shaped edging of gold and pearl bead which was repeated down the front of the jacket.

Her only jewellery consisted of earrings, and even now she still marvelled at her luck in finding the large circles of gold and pearl beads that matched the decoration on the dress so perfectly. High-heeled gold strappy sandals completed the outfit, and as she picked up her French gold beaded evening bag she felt a sudden panic at the thought of being overdressed. But it was too late to change because Blair had knocked on the door.

He stepped into the living-room, then stood looking at her in silence. His well-cut suit was more formal than the usual run of menswear, his bow-tie giving it the effect of evening apparel. 'You look wonderful,' he said at last, his deep voice holding a low note which did nothing to conceal his genuine admiration.

'I've already told her that much,' Max said briefly, then added with a grin, 'I'm glad others can see it as well.'

'You'll be late for Rotary,' Lynn warned him hastily, then turned to Blair as her grandfather made his departure. 'I was afraid I might be too dressed up.'

'You'll grace the dining-room beautifully. We're eating in there this evening.'

The approval in his eyes sent a glow of pleasure through her, but she managed to say calmly, 'Don't you always use the dining-room?'

'No. It gives Maisie extra work, but I've decided the time is drawing near when it will be used more often.'

'Really? When will that time be?' she queried.

But he offered no further explanation. Instead he said, 'In the meantime Maisie, Bert and Sandra have their meals at regular hours in the kitchen. However, tonight is a special occasion.'

'Special? Why would that be?' she probed.

'Tonight is your first meal at Marshlands. I've told Maisie it's to be like a family gathering.'

'Are you saying your parents will be there?'

'No. Taupo is too far away to make a trip for a meal. I'm afraid I don't see much of them, therefore I've come to look upon Bert and Maisie as family.'

The regret in his voice caused her to look at him with sudden insight. 'I believe you miss contact with your own family.'

'Yes. I'll admit I consider the family unit to be important. In fact, I envy large families.'

The words told her something about him, and they also gave her a reason for his special care of Tony. The little boy was his cousin's child, therefore he was family. And then another question leapt into her mind, causing her to ask casually, 'Is Sandra also part of the family circle?'

'Sandra hasn't been with me for as long as Bert and Maisie,' he informed her easily, then changed the subject by saying, 'Shall we go? Where's your woollen wrap?'

'It's here.' She picked up the handwoven cream cape she had worn to the arts and crafts exhibition.

He took it from her, and, as on that previous occasion, he placed it about her shoulders. His fingers touched her neck gently while adjusting the collar, then lingered on the rise of her breast as he attended to the diagonal line of buttons.

'This is an elegant garment,' he observed. 'It has a definite country air about it.' His fingers left the region of her breast, moving back to her neck where they stroked the smoothness of her jaw.

The touch of his fingers caused her throat to feel constricted, forcing her to remain standing transfixed before him. Her face was uplifted, and her heart began to thump while waiting for him to lower his lips to her own. But he failed to do so, and she found herself struggling against the let-down of anticlimax.

Had he known she'd been waiting to be kissed? she wondered while fighting an inner chagrin. Was disappointment written all over her face? If so he gave no sign of having noticed anything untoward as he opened the door and led her out to the car, which stood waiting on the drive.

Little was said during the short journey to the homestead, but as they turned in at the Marshlands entrance
Lynn became aware of strange contradictions plaguing
her mind. She had looked forward to this evening with
such happy anticipation, so why did her instinct now
warn her against hoping for too much? Was it because
Blair had failed to take the opportunity to hold her in
his arms?

The house on the hill breathed an air of welcome with
lights shining in its upper windows and from the lounge
and open front door, yet she continued to be assailed
by a vague unease. Brushing it aside, she told herself it
was merely a fit of jittery nerves, and, while she knew
she had nothing to fear from Maisie's attitude towards
herself, she realised that Sandra would be polite only
because Blair was present.

He parked the car near the concrete steps leading up
to the front porch, then led her into the hall. Maisie
appeared as if by magic, her round face smiling
pleasantly. She took Lynn's cape and laid it on a large
ornately carved chest made from camphor wood, then
turned to Blair. 'Bert has a lovely fire burning in the
lounge, and there's time for you to give Lynn a couple
of sherries before dinner.'

'You and Bert will join us,' Blair said, his tone
sounding more like a command than an invitation.

'Yes—if you insist.' She turned to Lynn to say almost
apologetically, 'My Bert is very shy when he first meets
people.' She then disappeared in the direction of the
kitchen.

Blair ushered Lynn into a large room warmed by
flames leaping in the wide open fireplace. A glance
showed the furniture and ornaments to be of high quality,
and no sound was made as they moved over the thick
pile of the wall-to-wall carpet.

He went to a cabinet where he poured drinks, while
Lynn found herself drawn towards the large plate glass

window which gave a panoramic view over the darkening countryside. Moments later he was beside her, a
stemmed crystal glass of sherry in his hand. Offering it
to her, he said, 'Welcome to the homestead.'

'Thank you, but it's not my first visit—in case you've
forgotten,' she returned in a dry tone.

He ignored the significance of the remark as he said,
'Tell me if this sherry is to your liking.'

She took the glass from him, then examined the deep
rich gold of the sherry. 'It looks very potent.'

'Corbans rich cream aged in oaken casks,' he told her,
twirling his own glass and holding it to the light. 'It has
a good nose.'

'And is guaranteed to make me chatter indiscreetly?'
She smiled, taking a sip and recognising it to be a sherry
she enjoyed.

He regarded her gravely. 'I'm ready to listen to anything you have to say.'

She took another sip. 'That sounds as if you expect
a guilty confession of some sort.'

'I'm told that confession is good for the soul.'

'Wouldn't that depend upon the depth of the guilt?'
She looked at him thoughtfully as a sense of depression
began to steal over her, dragging forth an impulsive
question. 'Why do I get the feeling that Tony's passport
is still on your mind?'

He shrugged. 'I understand the hunt for it still goes
on. May I ask what makes it leap into your mind?' His
eyes became searching as they regarded her steadily.

She returned his gaze unflinchingly. 'You can call it
my female intuition. It says you still doubt me, despite
your assurance that you'd got over the suspicion.'

She turned away from him to continue staring through
the window, her earlier apprehension returning with this
evidence that he still lacked confidence in her. It hurt
more than she cared to admit, and she had no wish for
him to see the mistiness in her eyes.

He moved to stand closer to her, his hand resting upon her shoulder. 'There's a fine view from this window, but I'm afraid it's too dark for you to see it.'

She blinked rapidly, staring towards the west. 'I can at least see the lights of Waipawa, and beyond it there's a brilliant gold streak above the peaks of the Ruahines.' She turned her eyes towards the south. 'Across the river there's another sprinkle of lights.'

'That's Tapairu. It was once a well-populated Maori settlement, but the time came when the young people left it for the brighter lights of the city.' He paused, then added in a dry tone, 'So many people become bored with country life.'

She said nothing, sensing the dig at Delphine, then caught her breath as she felt his fingers tighten on her shoulder.

'Would you become bored with country life, Lynn?' The question came softly, his lips not far from her ear.

She shook her head. 'You're forgetting I have an occupation that thrives in the country. The fields are full of material for stories. Why do you ask such a question?' She held her breath, waiting for his reply.

But before he could say anything Maisie came into the room. She was followed by a short grey-haired man whom she introduced to Lynn as her husband, Bert Bates, and who came forward to shake hands with her. She noticed that Bert's bright blue eyes took in every detail of her appearance, and as they moved from Blair to herself she felt that despite his shyness he was observant.

Blair poured drinks for them, and as he did so Sandra made an entrance with Tony, her arm placed affectionately about the boy's shoulder in a motherly attitude.

However, Tony shrugged her hand away and ran across the room to Lynn. He flung his arms around her, then looked up into her face to complain in an aggrieved tone,

'Sandra wouldn't let me come till I'd eaten every *vegable* on my plate, and she gave me lots and lots.'

'At least I'm taking care of him,' Sandra said to Blair as though making an effort to drive this point home.

'Of course you are, Sandra,' Blair acknowledged. 'I'm sure you're doing your best and I'm grateful.' He then dismissed the subject of Sandra's duties by turning to Bert. 'I've just been telling Lynn that most of the young people have left the Maori settlement across the river. Too quiet for them.'

Bert nodded his grey head. 'I'd say that's a fact. All except Ada, of course. It's not too quiet for her.'

'You can't expect that poor girl to go far,' Maisie put in.

Lynn felt mystified. She looked from one to the other, then curiosity compelled her to ask, 'Who is Ada?'

'She's a statue made of Carrara marble,' Maisie explained. 'She stands in the church cemetery over the grave of a young woman named Ada Maihi who died in 1912. I'm surprised you haven't been to see it.'

Bert said, 'After her death her parents sent a photo of her to craftsmen in Italy, the order being a life-sized statue of her. It's a beautiful piece of work.'

'The blouse and long skirt she's wearing were the fashion in those days,' Maisie said.

Sandra turned to Blair, her expression anxious as she said, 'I've promised to take Gary over to Tapairu to see the statue. You don't mind if I...if I go out with him...?'

Blair's voice held surprise. 'Of course not. Why should I mind?'

'I—I was just making sure,' Sandra said meekly. 'You see, Gary is always so sweet to me, and he's new to this district.'

Lynn looked at her wonderingly. Was Sandra hoping to raise a spark of jealousy in Blair? But the question was swept aside as Tony began tugging at her skirt.

The little boy regarded her seriously, then demanded in a clear voice. 'Lynn—please may I watch you do ogling?'

Puzzled, she looked at him in silence. *Ogling?* What on earth could he be talking about? 'I'm afraid I don't understand what you mean,' she assured him in a perplexed voice.

'Sandra told Maisie that you kept ogling Gary. I want to see how you do ogling,' he persisted, hopping with impatience.

A small gasp escaped Sandra as she snapped, 'Be quiet, Tony.'

The boy swung round to stare at her. 'You did so say she kept ogling Gary,' he accused defiantly. *'You did so!'*

Lynn forced herself to utter a light laugh. It was an attempt to brush the matter aside, but when she turned to Blair she found no answering amusement on his face. Instead his expression caused her spirits to sink because it held serious questions. He had seen her talking to Gary, and it seemed as if he believed what Sandra had said.

Nor did he offer comfort when, after explaining to Tony the meaning of the word ogle, he added, 'Lynn's eyes are guaranteed to knock some people sideways—at least when they first meet her. You'll understand when you grow up.'

Part of this last statement hit her with force, sending her spirits to an even lower level. 'When they first meet her,' he'd said. Did this mean that he himself had been knocked sideways, but that he had now overcome that phase of temporary insanity? Was he trying to tell her that their kisses had taken place only during moments of lunacy?

She looked at him wonderingly, trying to fathom the answers to these questions, but his expression had now become inscrutable. She sighed, realising that this evening would not prove to be one holding pleasant memories—and then the nail of distrust appeared to be hammered even further when he brought up the subject of Delphine.

His tone smooth, he asked, 'You've heard from overseas recently?'

'No. I've been told not to write again until I've been given a new address. I can only presume she's moving nearer her work.'

Sandra spoke casually. 'It's easy to guess you're referring to a certain party's mother. Nor will it be difficult for you to guess we're still searching for his passport.'

Lynn bristled at the veiled accusation, and in the tense silence that followed Sandra's words she fought to control her anger. As she did so she was struck by a thought that made her ask, 'Have you questioned Tony about it?'

Sandra sneered, 'Of course not. He's only six, and I doubt that he knows what is meant by a passport. Maisie and I have searched high and low, and that should be enough to prove it is nowhere to be found. It's been whipped off by an expert——'

Blair snapped angrily, 'That's enough, Sandra. You will not speak to our guest in that manner.'

Sandra sent him a disarming smile. 'I'm sorry, Blair—but you must realise I'm upset about this whole episode.' Her smile grew wider. 'Besides, you said that this was to be a family gathering, and families are always frank with each other.'

Maisie spoke sharply, her brown eyes troubled. 'That doesn't excuse rudeness, Sandra. You should apologise to Lynn.'

But Sandra maintained a sulky silence, and Lynn noticed that Blair made no attempt to draw an apology from her. Was he waiting to see what more could develop from Sandra's attack upon herself? Was he expecting the sherry to loosen her own tongue into a stream of confessions of guilt or admissions that she had taken the passport? He had already refilled her glass, perhaps with the hope that she would toss caution to the breeze.

She took a deep breath to control the nervous tension that was making her ready to scream, then she smiled as she questioned the boy. 'Do you know what a passport is, Tony?'

He nodded. 'Yes. It's a little book with no story in it. It's only gotta photo of me.'

Maisie was irritated. 'Well, now—will you just listen to that? When I asked him about it he just shook his head.'

Tony looked down at the floor. He shuffled his feet and said nothing while edging closer to Lynn.

She sensed his guilt. 'A little bird is whispering to me,' she said with a smile in an effort to gain his confidence.

'Are you sure it isn't a little frog?' Blair put in.

She ignored the remark as she continued to smile at Tony in a friendly manner. 'This little bird tells me you know where to find that passport. Will you tell Lynn the truth?'

'It's with a photo in my secret place,' he mumbled, then added more audibly, 'I've gotta have a secret place all my own.'

'Yes, of course, I understand,' Lynn assured him kindly. 'Tell me, why did you put these things in a secret place?'

'Because Sandra said she'd get rid of the photo with my mother and father in it. And the passport had a photo of me...'

'So you thought it was also in danger,' Lynn said.

Sandra exploded furiously. 'You little imp—where is it?'

'I'm not telling you my secret place!' Tony shouted at her.

'Of course not,' Blair agreed placatingly. 'Men must have their secrets. Now run and fetch them at once. I'd like to see them.'

Bert broke the silence following Tony's departure from the room. 'I know his secret place,' he informed them. 'He let it slip one day. Remember when he had a mouse in Dobbin's saddlebag? He told me he'd put a mouse in his secret place.'

'So that's where the passport has been all this time,' Maisie said, sending an indignant glare towards Sandra. 'I must say you didn't search very well. And you were so quick to blame Lynn,' she added reproachfully.

Bert appeared to be mystified. 'What's all this fuss over the lad's passport?'

Lynn betrayed her surprise. 'Didn't you *know*? I'm supposed to have *stolen* it.'

Maisie cut in, 'I didn't tell him because I didn't believe it.'

'Thank you, Maisie.' Lynn felt a surge of gratitude.

Moments later she held her breath as Tony returned to the room, the passport and wedding photo clutched in his hand. He gave them to Blair, who stared at them in silence, and watching them both she was unable to resist a cryptic remark. 'Perhaps you'll concede this particular round to me, Blair?'

'Yes—I think you can put a ring round that telling statement,' he admitted gravely. 'And I think this photo is the reason I thought I'd met you before. That cloud of flaming hair has stayed with me.'

'So that's another mystery cleared up.' She felt slightly hysterical. Giggles escaped her, erupting into laughter she found difficult to control while watching the unfathomable expression on Blair's face.

However, Blair's thoughtful silence had a different effect on Maisie, who stood up abruptly and spoke with decision. 'It's time Sandra and I attended to the meal,' she declared, then turned to her husband. 'Bert—perhaps you'll take a look at the dining-room fire. I'm sure Tony would like to help you carry a few pieces of wood,' she added as she left the room followed by Sandra.

Bert stood up. 'Coming, young fellow?' he invited.

The boy had settled himself on the mat before the fire. He looked up at Bert and said, 'No, thank you. I want to stay here beside Lynn.'

She spoke to him in a sorrowful voice. 'Poor Bert— he asked you to help him and you refused. I didn't think you'd refuse to help an old person—especially Bert.'

Tony thought about it for a few moments then scrambled to his feet. 'I suppose I've gotta do it,' he mumbled as he ran after Bert.

Blair sighed. 'Why can't Sandra handle him as you do?'

'Because at heart she's impatient with children— especially little boys like Tony.'

'But not big boys—like Gary?'

'I understand she likes to be with him,' Lynn said carefully.

'But you're not impatient with little boys?' he observed.

'Would I be writing for children if I were?' she pointed out.

'However, you must be thoroughly fed up with one particular... big boy,' he persisted.

'How right you are,' she commented decisively. 'I'm now regretting that I didn't come in my own car.'

He frowned. 'Are you saying you'd have left before dinner?'

'Well—soon after it. I wouldn't hurt Maisie by leaving before a meal she'd prepared for a guest. However, the manner in which you tolerated Sandra's rudeness towards me certainly made me feel like rushing home at once.'

'But now you're glad you didn't?' he queried.

'Yes—I'm glad because the mystery of the missing passport has now been solved. I'm really thankful about that.'

'Then perhaps you understand why I didn't blow my top at Sandra. I was hoping an answer of some sort might come out of it, although I didn't expect you to handle the situation so well.'

'It wasn't very difficult.'

His voice became soft, his eyes intense as they held her own. 'I suppose it's useless to admit that I regret any trauma it may have caused you?'

Her shoulders lifted in a slight shrug. 'That particular trauma was no worse than being accused of having plans to take Tony to his mother. Nor was it any worse than the attitude of suspicion you've constantly held towards me.'

'Is it necessary to tell you that those suspicions no longer exist?' His deep voice held sincerity.

'They don't? How interesting.' She sent him a bleak glance, and, having no intention of succumbing to the sympathy in his tone, she forced scepticism into her own.

Nor did it escape him. 'You feel unsure about that?'

'One can't be sure of anything round these parts,' she informed him abruptly. 'Nor can I help feeling that something else is sure to arise—something that will arouse your suspicions all over again.' An inner conviction that this would happen caused her to move restlessly, and, leaving her chair, she went to the window where she stood gazing across the darkness towards the lights of the Tapairu Maori settlement.

He crossed the room to stand beside her. His hand was on her shoulder, his head bent while he murmured in her ear, 'Get those thoughts out of your mind. You're meeting trouble even before it raises its head. Tomorrow I'll take you to see the statue of Ada Maihi.'

The freshness of his aftershave teased her senses, and although his words caused her heart to leap she forced herself to say, 'Thank you for the kind thought, but it won't be necessary. I'm sure I can find my way to Tapairu without too much trouble.'

His voice snapped crisply, 'Are you saying you've no wish to come with me?'

'You're reading the signs correctly,' she informed him calmly, her eyes still piercing the gloom beyond the window.

'The signs?' His hands on her shoulders turned her to face him. 'Kindly explain your reasons,' he commanded.

She met his gaze fearlessly, although her eyes were shadowed by an inner hurt. 'Well, to be honest, I'm not amused by the *constant* antagonism that arises between us. Nor do I appreciate your *constant* distrust.'

'Haven't I told you that all doubts have now flown——?'

'That's just the point, Blair. Those doubts shouldn't have been there in the first place, and, despite your assurance, they still lurk just below the surface. I *know* they are there. I can *feel* them.'

'I see.' His jaw tightened, but before he could deny her allegations Tony came running into the room with a message from Maisie. Dinner was ready and would they please go into the dining-room where everything was waiting to be served?

As they left the lounge Lynn knew a sudden despondency. Why couldn't she keep her mouth shut? Why couldn't she let past hurts bury themselves and make a new beginning? But that wasn't Lynn's way. She wanted the air really cleared.

She had also hoped that Blair would have at least tried to persuade her to visit the settlement across the river with him—but he had made not the slightest attempt to do so. It meant, of course, that he couldn't care less.

CHAPTER NINE

BLAIR ushered Lynn across the hall and into the dining-room, which was through the wall from the kitchen. Steaming dishes stood on mats placed to protect the mahogany table, and this was surrounded by matching chairs. He pulled out the one which seated her on his right, then took his place at the end of the table.

Maisie and Sandra were opposite Lynn, while Bert sat beside her. Only Gary was missing, but apparently he was out visiting friends. She knew that these people were Blair's servants, yet it was obvious he did not treat them as such. A family gathering, he had said. Tonight we eat in the dining-room. Even Tony was permitted to stay up later than usual.

It was then that Lynn realised that she was being honoured, although at times the agreeable atmosphere of the evening had almost flown out of the window. Nevertheless the pleasure of sitting beside Blair at his table was not to be denied, and she became aware of the quiet satisfaction that filled her. Satisfaction? No—it was more than that. It was verging so close to happiness she was afraid to examine it too closely.

Its effect caused her to brush the irritations of the past hour from her mind, and to chatter with animation. Tactfully, and without holding the floor, she drew the others into the conversation while telling them about her life in Wellington, and the tasks involved while working in her father's surgery.

She knew that Blair watched her intently, a half-smile playing about his lips, and she also suspected that Sandra's faintly bored air was deliberately displayed.

However, she did not allow this to provoke her until she explained that there were times when a child needed to be kept amused while its mother was being examined.

Sandra's sneer then became more evident. 'Are you trying to tell us you know how to entertain children?' she asked with derision.

Lynn refused to be drawn into open hostility; therefore she said smoothly, 'Believe it or not, there are occasions when I make an attempt to do so.'

Sandra was amused. 'Really? How do you begin?'

The question brought a sharp retort from Blair. His lips becoming tight, he turned cold eyes upon Sandra as he spoke icily. 'It might interest you to learn that Lynn is a published author of children's books.'

'*Children's* books?' Sandra refused to be impressed. 'Well, I suppose writing for the juvenile market should be easy enough. If Lynn can do it—I dare say anyone can.'

Lynn continued to remain unruffled. 'Quite correct,' she agreed. 'The writing is easy enough—but getting it published is a different matter altogether.'

Maisie said, 'I believe it's a specialised craft because of the words to be used for different age-groups.'

Bert grinned. 'Even simple words are beyond Sandra.'

'Are you hinting that I can't read?' Sandra bristled with anger.

'If you could you'd see the writing on the wall,' Bert drawled.

His words puzzled Lynn, although she heard them bring a chuckle from Blair. She also realised that Bert had said very little during the meal, yet she was well aware that his observant blue eyes had moved watchfully from Blair to herself. So what did he mean by 'the writing on the wall'? Had her face betrayed her inner feelings towards Blair? Or had Blair looked at her in such a way that Bert had imagined an alliance between them? But even as she waited for Bert to explain his words the ring of the telephone echoed in the hall.

Blair said, 'I'll answer it in my office.' He stood up and left the room, his departure seeming to denude it of a vital presence.

Sandra then turned to attack Bert. 'I want to know what you meant by saying I can't read——'

'Work it out for yourself,' he snapped.

'That'll do, Bert,' Maisie said, then turned to Lynn. 'You are fortunate to have such a hobby. It's a pity a certain party's mother couldn't have had a similar interest.' Her words ended with a sigh as she sent a glance towards Tony, who sat on the mat before the leaping flames in the open fireplace.

Lynn hesitated, then told them a little about her association with Delphine, and how it was through this friendship that she had become published. Then her words trailed away to silence as Blair came to the door.

'Stan is on the phone,' he announced, then spoke to Tony. 'Come and talk to Daddy—he's in London.'

Maisie beamed. 'Well, isn't that *wonderful*? Fancy talking to someone in *London*,' she exclaimed as Tony sprang to his feet and followed Blair.

They returned a short time later, Tony shouting with excitement. 'I talked to my daddy—I talked to my daddy—he's coming home!'

Blair added, 'He's searching for Delphine but has been unable to find her.' He looked directly at Lynn. 'Didn't you say something about a change of address?'

'Yes—but she hasn't given me one. At least, not yet.'

Sandra put in acidly, 'Perhaps she knows Stan is searching for her and has no wish to be found.'

'Sheer supposition,' Bert argued, sending a cool glare towards Sandra.

After that the conversation became general. Sandra put Tony to bed while Maisie cleared the table. Lynn tried to help her but was led back to the lounge by Blair where they stood before the glowing embers of the fire, yet despite its warmth the atmosphere between them seemed to have cooled.

Searching for a reason, Lynn blamed the phone call from London. It had put Blair into a morose mood which was making their relationship so strained that she could almost sense the spectres of Stan and Delphine hovering above their heads. And this was proved to be a fact when his scrutiny became penetrating.

'You're sure you've no idea of Delphine's new address?'

She noticed the hardness in his voice. 'Quite sure.'

'Would you tell me if you did know?' He sounded sceptical.

'I see no reason to keep it from you. However, I must say I'm surprised to learn that Stan is seeking her whereabouts.'

'I suspect it's because he still loves her. It's possible he wants to bring her home.'

'Don't you mean he wants to whistle her to heel? He wants her to continue to be his *slave*.' Her voice held an edge to it because, despite her own reservations, her sympathies were still with her friend.

He became irritable. 'No, I do not mean that at all.'

Surprise caused her to say, 'You're really anxious to see them together again?'

'Wouldn't it be better for the boy? Tony needs his own parents.'

'He needs parents who love each other,' Lynn pointed out. 'Do you think it's possible for Stan to change his attitude towards Delphine by being more understanding and less domineering?'

'I'd say anything is possible—from the sound of his voice on the phone,' Blair said thoughtfully.

'I can understand your sympathies being with your cousin,' she said, giving vent to a small sigh. 'Apart from a man seeing only a man's side of a problem, blood is thicker than water.'

'Which means you consider I'm totally one-sided,' he gritted.

Later when he drove her home the short journey was achieved almost in silence. At the cottage he left the driver's seat, then walked round the car and opened the door for her. As they stepped up on to the veranda he looked down into her face and said, 'I'm afraid this evening has had its ups and downs.'

'Maybe—but I enjoyed it. Thank you for inviting me to sit at your table.' She smiled up at him, her heart beating at a slightly faster rate. Was he about to kiss her goodnight?

He made no move to do so. Instead his face remained serious as he said, 'It was a sight that pleased me. One I'll remember.'

'Or is it one you're more likely to forget?'

'Why have you so little faith in me?'

'Perhaps because your lack of faith in me is apparent. You think I'm holding back on Delphine's address. I know you do. I can feel your doubts about me.'

He grabbed her shoulders and gave her a slight shake. 'That is your imagination entirely,' he declared, staring down into her face. 'I've a good mind to——' But before he could say more the deep-throated croak of a bullfrog rose on the still air. It was like a cue, causing Blair to say, 'I do believe that's Freddie taking his singing lessons.'

The giggle that escaped Lynn relieved her tension.

Blair took her hand and drew her towards the end of the veranda. 'Freddie is singing a song about the moon's glow on the water. It tells that now is the best time to walk round the lake.'

'I distinctly heard him say something about moonlight being dangerous. He also said I'm wearing the wrong shoes.'

'Then change them.' It was a cryptic command until he added, 'Unless you have no wish to walk in the moonlight with me.'

A walk in the moonlight with Blair? How could she resist? 'I'll be quick,' was all she said.

She also moved silently, hoping her grandfather would not be disturbed. His car in the garage gave mute evidence of his return from his Rotary meeting, and his darkened window indicated the possibility that he now slept. Therefore she tiptoed through the living-room to the laundry where she kept a heavier pair of shoes for wearing outside in the damp grass.

When she rejoined Blair he had left the veranda and stood waiting for her on the drive. He took her hand, his fingers entwining with her own to give a feeling of sweet intimacy, and together they walked towards the water. When they were within a few feet of it another croak came from the rushes growing near the edge.

The sound drew a comment from Blair. 'It's OK, Fred—we're taking your advice.'

His hand left hers but made its way up her arm while leading her across the soft damp ground where long grass caressed her ankles. On their right the shadowy hawthorns dropped white petals tinged with pink. On their left came an occasional plop into the water, or a flapping of wings from one of the lake's feathered residents.

They walked in silence, his hand continuing to hold her arm, its pressure through the wool of her cape giving her a sense of security. Even so the moon's rays, which lit the water while throwing eerie shadows into the surrounding valleys, made her feel they were in an enchanted hollow where dreams were made, and she feared that if she spoke the spell would be broken.

Was Blair wrapped in a similar fantasy? she wondered. Apparently not, because her illusions were shattered when he brought her back to reality by asking a mundane question. 'How do your stories progress?'

'I've been busy,' she admitted, then gave him a brief outline of her present work on the typewriter.

'It sounds suitable for the age-group.'

'I'm glad you think so. Normally I do not tell anyone about a story I have in mind.'

His hand tightened on her arm. 'Am I just anyone?'

The question caused her heart to leap, but she did not answer it. Instead she went on in a matter-of-fact voice, 'In some strange way the recounting of it tends to kill it.'

'Have you attempted any young adult stories yet? You know the sort of thing—boy meets girl, the inevitable quarrel and the happy making-up.'

'No.' The reply came abruptly.

'You're deliberately avoiding them?' His tone was teasing.

'Not exactly.'

'I believe you are. I'd even venture to say it's because you are not yet ready for them. You know so little about love.'

She laughed. 'While you are the great authority? You're still in the midst of sowing your wild oats.'

'I've been around,' he admitted nonchalantly. 'I could give you a few lessons.'

'Thank you, I—I don't think I need them,' she said faintly, her lips trembling. 'At least—not for the stories I'll be writing.'

'Nevertheless it's advisable to have a little knowledge sitting in the background,' he commented drily.

'Isn't a little knowledge supposed to be a dangerous thing?' she asked, misquoting a well-known poem.

'Only if one refuses to allow it to expand,' he pointed out.

His suppositions irritated her. 'You've no right to hint that my knowledge of romance needs to expand. I'm not completely naïve.'

'I doubt that your own personal history has seen much of it.'

Surprise caused her to look up at him. 'What makes you so sure about that? You make me sound as though I've never had a real boyfriend.' Her last words echoed her indignation.

'Well—have you?' His tone had become slightly mocking.

'That happens to be my own personal business,' she retorted.

'Something tells me your emotions could do with a sharp shot in the arm—an injection of emotional upheaval.'

'Administered by whom?' she queried derisively.

'By myself, of course. You could look upon me as Dr Blair.'

She laughed, falling in with his mood. 'Dr Blair, noted for his bedside manner! Something tells me the cure would be worse than the complaint—if you'll pardon me for saying so.'

'What makes you so sure about that?' He sounded nettled.

'Because doctors don't remain with one patient. They move away to other patients—if you get my point—which means that this one would be left lamenting.'

He was quick to pick up the last word. 'Really lamenting?'

'Only temporarily, of course,' she amended hastily, at the same time endeavouring to assure herself of this fact.

They had reached the end of the water where the fence barring their way caused them to turn and retrace their steps. As they did so the moonlight illuminated Blair's face, making Lynn acutely aware of his handsome features and the aura of vitality that radiated from every pore of his athletic form. It was a charismatic vapour that reached out to envelop her, silencing any protest she might have in mind as he drew her towards the shadows of the hawthorn trees where he took her in his arms.

Nor did she protest when his hand in the small of her back pressed her against his body and his head bent to find her lips. The heat of his palm through her clothes seemed to creep up her spine, causing her heart to thump and her pulses to race as she gave herself up to the joy of being in his arms.

But despite the ecstasy one small part of her brain remained cool, warning her that these were kisses without commitment. She was only the means of a temporary affair to Blair Marshall. Somebody new to the district— somebody who would be returning to Wellington, thus leaving him free.

Even so the deepening of his kiss sent her senses reeling, and of their own accord her arms reached to enfold him, finding their way to twine about his neck while her fingers fondled the hair at the back of his head. Her lips parted, her eyes closed and she became aware of a smouldering fire somewhere in the pit of her lower regions as his hand cupped her breast.

Her response caused his breath to quicken. He crushed her even closer to him, making no secret of his own inward fire and the depth of his longing. 'Lynn...Lynn...I want you,' he murmured, his lips trailing a line along her jaw. 'You know I want you?'

She nodded wordlessly.

'And I know you want me. Here and now. But the grass is too wet.' A sudden movement of his arms lifted her effortlessly, and, cradling her like a child, he carried her towards the cottage.

She was gripped by panic. Did he intend to stride into her bedroom? Had he forgotten her grandfather was just through the wall? But her fears were groundless. When they reached the veranda he set her down and said huskily, 'Goodnight, Lynn. I'll see you again...somewhere...some time.'

She stood in a daze, watching him go to his car. The lights blazed as he backed towards the road, then she stood immobile until the brilliant red tail-lights had disappeared round the first bend. 'Blair, oh, Blair... when will you come back?' she whispered to the surrounding darkness. Somewhere...some time, he'd said. It sounded so very remote—so very indefinite.

Sighing, she went inside, but despite her efforts to move silently Max's voice called to her when she went to the bathroom.

'Is that you, Lynn?'

'Yes, Grandy. I'm sorry if I disturbed you.'

'I wasn't asleep. I heard the car arrive some time ago. You took your time coming in.'

'Oh, well... we talked a little...'

There was a pause, then Max asked, 'Kissed you goodnight, did he?'

Her breath quickened at the memory, but her answer came casually. 'Yes, actually—he did.'

'Just a brief goodnight peck, was it?'

'Yes—something like that,' she lied.

'I don't believe you.' The retort that came through the wall was accompanied by a chuckle. 'You can't fool me, my girl. I've seen the way he looks at you.'

'Have you, Grandy? I can't say I've noticed anything special. When I do, you'll be the first to know. Now, goodnight.' The last words came firmly. She was not in the mood for further discussion with her grandfather, nor did she wish him to see her cheeks, which still felt warmer than usual.

Later, as she lay in her bed, her grandfather's words echoed in her thoughts. 'I've seen the way he looks at you,' he'd said. Was it possible that Blair's feelings for her were deeper than she realised? Did he love her, but refused to admit it even to himself? Was this because he had no intention of risking involvement with a city girl—

especially one who was friendly with Delphine? Birds of a feather, et cetera.

But what of herself? Did she love him? The answer hit her with force. Yes—she knew without a shadow of doubt that she loved him. Previously the suspicion had been pushed from her, but now she was ready to face it. She was ready to bring it out into the open and admit she'd found the man she wanted—the man with whom she longed to spend the rest of her life.

The knowledge gave her a feeling of warmth. Blair's face hovered above her in the darkened room as she relived the moments in the gloom of the hawthorn trees. A goodnight kiss? Oh, no—it had been much more than that, she told herself on a high wave of wishful thinking. The call to each other had been loud and clear, and possibly the time would come when the call would be answered. That would be the time when Blair was ready for commitment.

When she woke next morning the feeling of elation was still with her. A light song escaped her lips and the cottage was tidied in record time. The wholemeal scones were almost ready for the oven when her grandfather's voice spoke from behind her.

'I notice young Tony hasn't been near us lately. I suppose he's grown past the tadpole stage.'

'You're forgetting his pony,' Lynn said. 'He goes riding every day with Sandra. Last night I was told he's a natural on horseback; at least, that's what Sandra says.'

Last night. The mere mention of last night brought the memory of Blair's kisses crowding back into her mind, causing her to catch her breath. But that was last night. What of today? Would he come to see her?

'What are your plans for today?' Max drawled, almost as though reading her thoughts.

She felt he was watching her closely, therefore she kept her back turned to him. 'Oh, I suppose I'll spend it at the typewriter.'

'I thought you had something ready to post.'

'No, I ... I feel it needs a little more polishing.' No way would she go out today, she decided. Blair might come to see her. Surely last night's kisses meant something more than a casual embrace?

Filled with hope and anticipation, she spent the rest of the morning in the area of her room she now called her office, but as the hours passed into afternoon concentration became difficult. Her ears remained stretched for any sound that could herald Blair's approach, while every passing vehicle caused her to freeze as she listened for it to slow down. When none did, her work began to suffer.

By late afternoon she was fighting disappointment, and by the time she was preparing the evening meal she had accepted the fact that Blair had no intention of coming to see her. Or was he waiting until evening when the moon would again shine on the lake?

But the evening passed without a sign of him, and, gripped by a deep despondency, she realised that this was what had happened after he had kissed and held her closely on previous occasions. He had kept away from her. It was obviously his method of telling her she needn't expect too much involvement because it hadn't meant a thing. At least—not to him.

Max sensed her depression. 'So he didn't turn up today, huh?'

'You mean Tony?' she prevaricated with a forced smile. 'Didn't I tell you he rides Taffy every day after school?'

'You know I don't mean Tony,' he growled, then, as though making excuses for Blair, he went on, 'You must remember his days are fully committed to running a property.'

'And his nights?' The question slipped out.

Max shrugged. 'He's probably in his office. All good farmers keep records. They fill in a daily diary of the work being done, and they attend to their accounts.' He paused thoughtfully before asking, 'How is your own work progressing?'

'Not very well. I'm afraid it's in rather a chaotic jumble. I have several stories half finished because my mind keeps jumping from one to the other. I find myself doing a bit of this and a bit of that—which is really quite unlike my method of work.'

He eyed her shrewdly. 'That's because your mind is unsettled. It is not completely on your job. It's wandering over the fields in the direction of Marshlands.'

He was right and she knew it, but rather than admit to the truth of his accusation she said, 'Tomorrow I shall take myself firmly in hand. I shall return to my old system of taking one story at a time and getting it finished. I say it with my right hand raised.'

Max laughed. 'In other words you'll push that fellow out of your mind and get down to good solid work so that soon you really will have a packet to post.'

'That's right. Unless I send a ship out, it won't come home.'

Nor did she veer from this plan, and, although she longed for the sight of Blair's face and the sound of his deep voice, she saw and heard them only at the back of her mind. His continued absence caused an ache that sat like a lump of ice somewhere within the region of her heart, and in an attempt to override its cold depression she drove herself to a daily routine of work.

Her efforts resulted in the completing of all her half-finished stories, and seven days later she was rewarded by the sight of a packet ready to post to her publishers. It gave her a feeling of achievement, and despite the almost gale-force winds sweeping round the cottage she took it to town and handed it across the counter just before the mail closed.

Returning to the car, she glanced at the petrol gauge, then drove to the garage beside the bridge spanning the Waipawa river. The attendant filled the tank and also checked the oil, water and tyre pressures, and while he did so she left the car and went to gaze at the water flowing between the wide shingle banks.

The willows bordering the river, still bright with their spring green, were bent against the force of the wind, and beyond them the fields rose to higher ground. A few houses of the Tapairu settlement could be seen, and eye-catching among them was the small church, its white walls and red roof highlighted by the rays of the late afternoon sun.

The sight of it caused her to recall the evening at Marshlands when she had been told about the statue of Ada, and impulsively she decided to take the short drive to see it. There was no need to hasten home because it was Wednesday, which meant that Grandy would be having an evening meal at his Rotary Club meeting.

She paid for the petrol then left the garage to drive across the long bridge. A short distance beyond it a left-hand turn led her towards the higher ground of the Tapairu settlement, and within a few minutes she had stopped outside the church with its fenced enclosure of neatly kept graves.

Towering above them on a raised pedestal was the life-sized figure of Ada Erena Maihi, and although the engraved wording below her was in Maori, it was easy to understand that she had died in 1912 at the age of twenty-two.

Shadows were forming on the embroidered blouse with its gathered three-quarter-length sleeves, and in the folds of the long marble skirt from which peeped bow-topped shoes. Her left hand clasped a prayerbook against her breast.

Walking round the statue, Lynn saw that the thick wavy hair with its centre parting was worn in a coil at the back of the head. It would have been black, she thought, while the complexion would have been like coffee with cream. But it was the serenity of the face that caught and held her attention. Ada had been beautiful, she realised, feeling sure that the skilful Italian craftsmen had faithfully captured the good features and sweet expression from the photo sent by her parents.

But now she was home, where she stood in remote loneliness while all around her slept. Something of that same loneliness conveyed itself to Lynn, overwhelming her with a deep sadness that brought tears to her eyes. She tried to shrug it off by reminding herself that she was alive, and that she had her parents and Grandy. But she also knew they were not sufficient. She wanted Blair with an intense yearning, and she also knew that life would be nothing without him.

The knowledge caused her to stare at the statue through blurred eyes. 'What shall I do, Ada?' she whispered in a low voice. 'You came home but I...' She fell silent, gazing up at the marble face, then she took a deep breath as she went on, 'Thank you, Ada—I believe you've told me what to do. I'll go home. Perhaps the fact that I've had the car filled and checked is an omen. And, while I know Grandy will be disappointed to see me leave, he doesn't really need me now. Besides, I can't sit moping at Frog Hollow forever. So, just as you've come home to Tapairu, I'll go home to Wellington.' The resolve sent her hurrying back to the car.

Tears continued to trickle down her cheeks as she drove through the Waipawa township, and by the time she reached the cottage she was filled with even more determination. She would pack as soon as she'd lit the fire and had given herself a meal. Grandy would not be there to dissuade her, so the sooner she had her papers and clothes in her cases, the better.

Yet despite these intentions she found herself in no hurry to begin, and, after preparing a light meal, which she found difficult to swallow, she dragged her suitcases from where they lay hidden under the bed. Further, the more she put into them, the more concerned she became over what reason she should give her grandfather for her sudden departure.

She was still mulling over this particular problem when the phone rang, its shrill peal echoing through the cottage in a demand to be answered. Her heart leapt with a wild hope that it would be Blair ringing her at last, and she almost fell over one of the cases in her rush towards the living-room.

Day after day during the past week she had listened for a phone call from him, but it had not come, and now her hand almost shook as she lifted the receiver. Nor was her voice quite steady as she said, 'Hello?'

But the voice that floated over the line held nothing of Blair's resonant tones. It was a feminine voice, which said, 'Is that you, Lynn? It's Delphine.'

She was gripped by shock, and then amazement overrode her disappointment. '*Delphine?* Where are you? In London?'

'No, I'm in Napier. How is Tony? Is my little boy all right?'

'He's fine as far as I know, although I haven't seen him during the past week. Blair bought him a pony which he rides every day. Are you making a trip to see him?'

'More than that. I've come home.' The words were accompanied by a happy laugh.

Again Lynn could scarcely believe her ears. 'You mean—home to Stan?'

'I mean *with* Stan. He's here with me.' She named a motel. 'He came all the way to London to find me, and he's brought me home. Lynn—we're together again.'

'That's marvellous. Del, I'm so glad. I hope it will work out this time.'

'Oh—it will. This time everything is going to be different.' Delphine's voice rang with confidence.

'Are you saying he'll allow you to take a job?' Lynn tried to keep doubt from her voice.

'Actually I'll be working at home. Instead of assessing manuscripts written by other people I'll be working on my own. I've taken up writing romance.'

'That's wonderful. I hope you'll find success.'

'Would you believe I'm already on the way? The first has been accepted, the second is being assessed, and now I'm working on my third romantic novel. All this despite the daytime job I've had.'

Lynn felt excited for Delphine. 'Tell me, how did you get started on romance?'

'I tried it as a means of combating the troubles that assailed me every evening. During the first few weeks in my parents' home I was terribly unsettled in my mind. I suppose I was fretting for Tony. I was in a turmoil at having left him.'

'Yes, I understand.' She herself was in the throes of having her own private turmoil.

'It was my mother who suggested I should be doing something to channel my thoughts, and that it was time I tried writing my own manuscripts.' Delphine paused to laugh. 'You've heard the old saying about mother always knowing best? For the first time in my life I listened to her, and it has certainly paid off.'

'Stan won't mind your interest being tied up with heroes and heroines?' Lynn asked, recalling Stan's possessiveness.

Delphine giggled. 'He's delighted. Believe it or not, he's promised to set me up with the latest word processor, although I don't really need more than my portable typewriter.'

A question leapt into Lynn's mind. 'Does Blair know about all this and—and that you and Stan are together again?'

'Not yet. We've tried to phone him but their line seems to be out of order. Stan says the trouble will have been caused by one of those oaks or elms growing near the place where the line comes on to the property. Have you had a high wind?'

'Yes. It was blowing a gale this afternoon. Perhaps they don't even know it is out of order.'

Delphine's voice became urgent. 'Lynn, would you be a dear and do something for us—like taking a message?'

'Yes—of course.'

'Would you please go to Marshlands and tell Blair we're home? Tell him our plane got in this afternoon and that we'll drive home in a rental car tomorrow morning. Would you mind?'

Lynn caught her breath. Would she mind grasping at a legitimate excuse to go to Blair? 'I'll go at once,' was all she said.

'Thank you, Lynn—see you tomorrow,' Delphine said gratefully.

Lynn cradled the receiver, her thoughts in a whirl as she realised that Delphine and Stan were together again. They would be home tomorrow, but what sort of reception would her friend receive from the Marshlands household? Would she be made to feel an outcast?

Blair, she felt sure, would welcome her for Tony's sake, and also because Stan wanted her to be there as his wife. Maisie and Bert would be pleased to learn that the marital problem was being resolved in a satisfactory manner—but what would be Sandra's attitude?

No doubt her job of caring for Tony would be at an end, but Blair would probably consider that Maisie still needed her help in the house—therefore everything would go on as usual, except that she herself would not be there to see Tony living happily with his own parents.

But now the message must be delivered to Blair, the thought causing her to hasten towards the mirror and again almost tripping over a suitcase. She put a touch of lipstick to her mouth and raked a comb through the mass of unruly hair that had become windblown at Tapairu. The safety screen was placed before the open fire, and moments later she was driving to Marshlands.

As she approached the homestead she saw Maisie pacing the front veranda. The sight of her gave Lynn an apprehensive feeling that all was not well, and as she parked near the steps Maisie hurried to meet her.

The older woman reached the car almost before Lynn had unbuckled the seatbelt, her agitation more than obvious. 'Have you news?' she queried anxiously. 'Blair and Sandra have just arrived back, but Bert and Gary are still searching for him out there.' Her gaze wandered towards the fields.

Lynn looked at Maisie's pale face and tear-blurred eyes. A chill gripped her as she realised that something must be terribly wrong. 'What do you mean? Searching for whom?'

'For Tony, of course. He went riding with Sandra and—and somehow she lost him.'

'Lost him? That's ridiculous,' Lynn exclaimed.

'Well, that's what she says. You'd better come inside.'

CHAPTER TEN

WHEN Lynn entered the lounge she found the atmosphere charged with anxiety. Blair was pacing restlessly, the worried frown on his brow darkening as he stared at her in silence.

Sandra was also there, huddled on the settee, an occasional sniff being heard as she dabbed at tears. At the sight of Lynn she sprang to her feet. *'You!'* she shrieked. 'I told them it was *you*. What have you done with him? Where is he?'

Lynn made an effort to remain calm. 'If you're referring to Tony, I'm afraid I haven't a clue.'

'You're lying... I know you're lying,' Sandra spat.

Maisie spoke quickly. 'Don't be too hasty, Sandra.'

'Shut up, Maisie—don't be so obtuse.' Sandra turned on the older woman in a fury. 'She's taken him somewhere—I *know* she has. Didn't I go searching for him at Frog Hollow? Didn't I find her conspicuous by her absence? I'm telling you, she's got him tucked away somewhere.'

Blair had been watching Lynn, and he now moved to stand before her. Gripping her shoulders he stared down into her face. 'Is this true?' he demanded, his tone crisp.

The hardness in his voice shocked her. It made her feel cold. 'Is this what you believe?' she snapped back at him while shrugging his hands away.

'I'm afraid I don't know what the hell to believe,' he admitted.

'I suppose you know your phone is out of order,' Lynn said, hoping that the mundane remark would help to make her feel less agitated within herself.

171

'That much I do happen to know, although I've only recently become aware of the fact.' His voice was still cool. 'I tried to phone the police to report that Tony is missing, but our line was dead. I'd better go and see them about arranging a search-party——'

Sandra cut in angrily. 'Take *her* with you. Make them question *her*. See that they drag it out of her.'

'That's enough, Sandra,' Blair rasped. 'You're becoming hysterical.'

Maisie appealed to Sandra. 'Please try to keep calm. When I saw Lynn arrive I hoped she might know something about——'

'Of course she knows *plenty*,' Sandra cut in, her voice still raised. Then, swinging round to take a step nearer Lynn, she demanded rudely, 'So what do you want? Why have you come here?'

There was a sudden silence as they waited for Lynn's answer, and as she regarded each face in turn she realised that this was a most inappropriate moment to deliver such a message. Maisie's eyes held curiosity, Sandra's were filled with malice, while Blair's expression had become inscrutable.

Hesitantly, she said, 'Actually I . . . I've come to tell you that Tony's mother is in Napier——'

Sandra broke in with a shriek of triumph. 'There, now—what did I say? Of course she's whipped him off to Napier. I told you so . . . *I told you so* . . .'

Lynn opened her mouth to say that Stan was there also, but before she could utter a word Blair's cold voice hit her ears.

'Is this the truth?' he demanded.

Lynn's chin rose as she glared at him with disdain. 'Again I ask—is this what you believe?'

He frowned. 'Can you give me an assurance that it is not the truth?'

She continued to face him defiantly. 'Do you need it? Have you so little faith in me?' A deep hurt caused her words to tumble bitterly.

There was a tense silence while he took a deep breath, then he surprised her by saying, 'Forgive me—I've been almost out of my wits with worry. Of course I have faith in you. I do not believe you've had anything to do with the boy's disappearance.'

His words sent Sandra's fury to new heights, and, tossing caution to the breeze, her raised voice stormed, 'Don't let that innocent look fool you, Blair—just let me get the truth out of her.' There was a swift movement as one of her hands grasped a fistful of Lynn's hair, while the long fingernails of her other hand clawed to draw blood from Lynn's cheek.

Lynn screamed as she tried to leap away, but the grip on her hair held fast. She heard Maisie's gasp of horror, and she knew that Blair had wrenched Sandra's hand from her head while flinging the blonde girl to the floor.

'You bitch!' he snarled, snatching a clean handkerchief from his breast pocket and holding it to Lynn's cheek.

She felt his arms tighten about her, and leaning against him she began to weep, sobbing against his shoulder.

Sandra's voice came sneeringly from where she lay on the floor. 'Watch it, Blair. You're running a risk.'

He ignored the comment as he rested his cheek against Lynn's forehead while holding her even closer.

Sandra's derisive tones came again. 'You're besotted by her red hair and green eyes. She's thrown out a net and you'll be caught—which is something you've been avoiding for years.'

Blair looked down into Lynn's face. 'I'm afraid the warning comes too late. It's possible I've already been caught,' he murmured in her ear.

She heard the words as in a dream, then warned herself against taking them seriously. Blair was merely being kind. He was just offering comfort after the attack by Sandra.

But despite the presence of the others his arms remained about her as he whispered, 'Darling—I'm truly sorry for the treatment you've received in this house.'

Lynn caught her breath as her heart leapt. Was she hearing correctly? Had he actually called her darling? Words evaded her as she looked up at him wonderingly.

And then Maisie was beside them with a Dettol-soaked cloth which Blair took and held to Lynn's cheek. He wiped the torn flesh gently, then returned the cloth to Maisie. After that his arms went about Lynn again while he pressed her head against his shoulder.

Lynn stood still, afraid to break the spell that seemed to have descended upon her. She knew that Maisie watched with an interested gleam in her eye, and that Sandra had raised herself from the floor to the settee.

The blonde girl's manner had become sulky as she demanded in derisive tones, 'Is this supposed to be a love scene? Are you forgetting there's a small boy out there waiting to be found? Shouldn't you both be out searching?'

Maisie sighed as she spoke to Blair. 'Bert and Gary have just come in. They say there's no sign of the boy or his pony.'

Sandra sneered, 'Of course there isn't. Haven't I told you where he is? He's in Napier with his mother. *She* took him there——' Her words were silenced by the sound of a vehicle approaching the homestead.

Blair went to the window, then exclaimed, 'It's Bill Jordon with his horse trailer. He's got Tony and Taffy with him.' He hurried from the room followed by Lynn and Maisie, and, reluctantly, by Sandra, who lagged in the rear.

Bill Jordon was quite unaware of the relief caused by his arrival. He stood waiting while Gary and Bert unloaded the pony from the trailer, and as they led it away to the stable he spoke to Blair. 'My wife tried to phone you, but your line appears to be out of order. It seems that this young fellow decided to take a ride on the road, and you can guess what happened. Taffy headed for his old home and the boy wasn't strong enough to control him.'

'We're more than thankful to see him,' Blair admitted. 'Will you come in?'

'No, thank you. I must go home. Incidentally, Tony has had a meal. My wife gathered the impression that he was starving.'

Blair thanked him again and they watched the car and trailer leave the yard.

Sandra spoke briskly. 'Come along, Tony, there's time for a bath before bed.'

Blair cut in. 'But first we'll have a short chat. Why did you go on the road, Tony? You know it's forbidden.'

The boy hung his head then admitted, 'I got tired of waiting for Sandra. She was a long time.'

Sandra became agitated. 'Please let me put him to bed. He's very tired after... after so much excitement.'

'All in good time,' Blair drawled. 'There's something here I don't quite understand.' He turned to Tony. 'Tell me why you were waiting for Sandra. I thought you were out riding with her.'

Tony nodded vigorously. 'Yes, but she went into Dad's house with Gary. She told me to wait outside, and I waited and waited...'

Blair sent a swift glance towards Sandra. 'Ah, light begins to dawn. So what happened?'

'After a long time I got tired of waiting so I went inside to find her. She was on the bed with Gary. They were kissing——'

Sandra drew a sharp breath then spat, 'You little wretch—— '

Tony went on, 'So I thought I'd have a ride on the road while she wasn't looking—but when I tried to turn

Taffy round he wouldn't stop. He trotted faster and faster. He went on and on until...'

'Until he reached his old familiar pastures,' Blair concluded for the boy. He paused thoughtfully before turning to Maisie. 'I think the picture is fairly clear. Perhaps it would be wiser for you to put Tony to bed this evening. I've a few words to say to Sandra.'

Tony began to protest. 'I want Lynn to put me to bed——'

But Lynn heard only his last words as she slipped unobserved into the hall and made her way to her car. She had no wish to hear what was about to pass between Blair and Sandra, and within a few minutes she was driving home.

'Darling', he'd called her. The memory made her heart sing until she realised it sounded like the prelude to another loving interlude between them. But like the others it would fizzle out and end in nothing—therefore it was one she'd be wise to avoid. Depression then descended to wrap her in the gloomy knowledge that the sooner she packed and left for Wellington the wiser she'd be. Tears filled her eyes, blurring the swathe of headlights cutting the darkness that had now fallen.

When she reached the cottage she examined her face beneath the bright light of the bathroom mirror. The scratches were still sore, but looked worse than they felt although Sandra's nails had left three long red lacerations. She bathed them again, then tried to shrug the blonde's action from her mind.

After dabbing her cheek with a towel, she removed the screen from the open fire, threw more wood on the glowing embers, then continued with her packing. At the same time she felt thankful that Grandy would be home later than usual because this evening also included an extra inter-club meeting to be held after the main function.

However, she was not prepared for the sound of a car within the next few minutes, and when she heard the french door open she presumed the inter-club meeting must have been cancelled. But it was not Max who had walked into the cottage and now stood regarding her from the bedroom doorway. It was Blair.

'What are you doing?' he demanded without preamble or apology for having walked in uninvited.

She swallowed as she said, 'Can't you see for yourself?'

'You appear to be packing your bags with the intention of leaving.'

She nodded, feeling too miserable to speak.

He regarded her seriously. 'May I ask why?'

She turned away before he could see the mistiness in her eyes, then, evasively, she said, 'Grandy's much better now. He no longer needs me to be around.'

His voice hardened. 'Aren't you really saying you've become bored with country life? You're now beginning to miss the bright lights and the company of your friends.'

'No—I am not,' she flared angrily.

'Max is at Rotary, I presume. Does he know you're leaving?'

'Well, no... not yet.'

'Don't tell me you intend skipping off before he gets home?'

'Of course not—but I'll leave first · thing in the morning.'

He watched her take undies from a drawer and stuff them into the corners of her case, then queried lazily, 'Is it permissible to ask what has brought about this sudden decision?'

Irritation welled within her. 'How would you know it's a sudden decision? You haven't been near to know what plans I've made.' It was impossible to keep the reproach from her voice.

He looked at her closely. 'You've missed me?'

'Of course I missed you.' She almost choked with fury at having made such an admission.

'So you came searching for me this evening?' The question came softly as he took a step nearer and stared down into her eyes.

'Certainly not. The day I go searching for a man will be the day! I came with a message—if you care to remember.'

'Oh, yes—something about Delphine being in Napier.'

She took her jeans from the wardrobe, folded them carefully and placed them in her suitcase. Then, as she lifted jerseys from their hangers, she said, 'I was prevented from delivering the entire message. I was to tell you she'd be here tomorrow in a rental car.'

He shrugged. 'I'll tell Maisie.'

'Our phone is not out of order, so if you'd care to ring her you're welcome to do so.'

'I have no wish to ring Delphine, thank you.'

'But perhaps you'd like to phone Stan. He's in Napier with her.' The words were spoken casually.

'*Stan?* Why didn't you say so when you were at Marshlands?'

'I was about to do so when I was interrupted with some force—*if* you care to remember,' she repeated.

'Will I ever forget?' He moved nearer to examine the scratches on her face, his eyes kindling with anger.

His nearness caused a tremor to pass through her, and moving away she said, 'So—do you wish to speak to him?'

'No. Tomorrow will be soon enough for him to tell me how long Delphine is staying.'

'That is something I can tell you here and now. He's brought her home. They're together again.' She went on to tell him of Delphine's success in the field of writing romance. 'So, you see—it will be different this time.' Lynn sighed as a twinge of envy niggled with her feeling of happiness for her friend.

'Let's hope it'll last this time.' His tone echoed scepticism.

'You haven't much faith in people.' The accusation came from her with vehemence.

'What makes you so sure about that?'

'Personal experience, of course,' she flashed at him.

He moved swiftly to grab her shoulders, his manner changing to one of dominance as he glared down into her face. 'Now, you listen to me. Any doubts I ever had concerning your intentions towards young Tony no longer exist. Do you understand?'

She nodded then said, 'What I don't understand is why they existed in the first place.'

He stared at her for several long moments before he said, 'I think—because I was afraid of you.'

She laughed. '*You*—afraid of *me*? That's a joke.'

'Not when you consider I feared your power to change my life.'

Her pulses began to race. 'How could I change your life?'

But instead of uttering the words she longed to hear, he said, 'When Sandra voiced suspicions concerning your intentions towards Tony, I grasped at them as being good enough reasons to keep you at arm's length.'

'But you didn't . . . keep me at arm's length.'

'No. You're a fairly powerful magnet. And now I'd like to have my mind cleared about this abrupt departure. You still haven't told me why you're leaving tomorrow morning.'

She raked in her brain for an answer. How could she admit that her love for him was making her own situation unbearable? It seemed distressingly easy for him to make her imagine she meant the world to him—and then to completely ignore her existence, but now she had reached the stage of not being able to take any more of it.

'Well?' he demanded impatiently.

'Ada told me to go home,' she admitted inanely.

'*Ada?* Who the devil is Ada?'

'Ada Maihi. I went to see her statue at Tapairu. She said that . . . feeling as I do . . . I'd be wise to go home . . .' She stopped, appalled by the admission that had slipped out. But perhaps he hadn't noticed.

He had noticed. The grip on her shoulders became firmer and his voice acquired a sudden tension. 'It's a pity Ada couldn't have put you wise to a few other facts.'

'Oh? Such as?' She looked at him wonderingly.

'Such as the fact that you mean everything in the world to me.'

Her heart leapt. Did he realise what he'd said? Then she shook her head as she said, 'I wouldn't have believed her.'

'Why not?'

'Because if that were true you yourself would have told me. You wouldn't have left it to Ada.'

His hands moved from her shoulders and his arms encircled her body. 'I'm telling you now.'

Her pulses began to race as she asked, 'Would Ada have also told me why you kept away—why you followed the tactic of kissing me and then galloping out of sight?'

'She'd have explained that I needed to be sure of myself, and of you. She would have reminded you that I had the example of Stan and Delphine constantly before me, to say nothing of the fear that you, also, could tire of country life.'

'Aren't you forgetting that most of my inspiration comes from country life?'

'At least that thought has been a comfort.' His gaze became thoughtful as it returned to the half-filled suitcases. 'But now I'm puzzled by your determination to rush away from the scene of these inspirations—especially with Delphine's return so close at hand.'

She leaned against him, revelling in the feel of his arms holding her against his body, and in the faint aroma of his aftershave. The desire to go home had vanished.

He went on, 'Won't she be disappointed to discover you've left without seeing her? Especially as she knows you're here.'

'Yes, I suppose so.'

'Then why rush away before she gets here? Why not delay your departure for a few days? It'll help Max to become used to the fact that your visit has almost ended.'

'Yes—perhaps I'd better do that.' She grasped at these excuses that enabled her to change her mind without going into further explanations of her true reason for leaving.

'Good girl,' he murmured, his finger tilting her chin upward.

She closed her eyes, waiting for his kiss, then felt his lips trail across her forehead, resting briefly upon her closed lids. Her breath quickened as they found her mouth, then the world stood still as his kiss deepened.

At last he paused to whisper huskily, 'Darling...'

Her heart sang. There it was again—*darling*. She waited in a state of tension, listening for the words that would say he loved her, but his mouth returned to hers while his arms held her even more closely against him.

He paused again. 'I'm glad you'll stay to welcome Delphine. I'll tell Maisie we must all do our best to make her feel wanted at Marshlands. The past must be forgotten. It must not raise its head to ruin their new beginning.'

'I'm sure Maisie will agree. Let's hope Sandra will also agree on that point.' She was becoming conscious of frustration. Had he no intention of telling her he loved her?

His eyes rested upon the scratches marring Lynn's cheek, then his words came crisply. 'Sandra will have to go. She'll no longer be necessary to care for Tony, who will return to live with his parents in the manager's house.'

'Maisie will miss her help in the house,' Lynn pointed out.

'I doubt it. I've already decided who will fill her place. Maisie has a cousin with whom she has a good relationship. I've met her several times, and as she's in need of a live-in position the job will be offered to her.'

'Maisie will be delighted.'

'I hope so. I feel sure they'll be happy running Marshlands together.'

His last words were spoken casually, yet they swamped Lynn with a devastating chill as she realised they could have only one meaning. Blair had no intention of making her his wife. Marriage was the last thought he had in mind, therefore this closeness—these kisses—meant nothing to him. They were merely a passing whim.

This seemed to be proved by the fact that while holding her in his arms his thoughts were not really with her. They were with Stan, Delphine and young Tony, and their future life together. They were with Maisie and her cousin—and the running of Marshlands. It seemed clear that his thoughts were anywhere but with herself, and as the knowledge sank in and registered more firmly it brought a feeling of desolation.

Yet, knowing these facts, she lacked the power to disengage herself from his arms, and, although she told herself she was being a weak fool, she savoured the joy of resting her head against his broad shoulder. And when he bent his head again, searching for her lips, her arms crept up to encircle his neck while she responded with more ardour than she realised.

A sudden movement of his arms swept her up to be cradled like a child, and in a daze she felt herself being laid on the bed. His length was stretched beside her in a flash, and she revelled in the feel of her breasts being crushed against his chest. Nor was she able to control the delicious sensations surging through her body, and when his hand moved beneath her jersey the feel of his thumb stroking her taut nipple drew a small gasp from her.

'Darling...darling...I want you,' he murmured huskily against her lips. 'I know you want it too...'

They were not the exact words she longed to hear, yet their truth was undeniable. She knew he wanted to make love to her, and that inside her own body a smouldering fire was about to burst into flame. It was a shared need too deep to ignore.

'Let us be together—here and now,' he whispered.

'Here and now.' The words echoed in her brain to clear her confused thinking. If she consented, that was all it would ever be. Here and now. And later? Nothing—apart from desolation. Yet it would be almost worth it to have been possessed by Blair.

A low groan escaped him as he moved against her, then he froze as the cottage walls were pierced by a series of shrill, demanding blasts of a car horn. The sound sent them both springing from the bed, a muttered oath escaping Blair as he said, 'That'll be Max. I'm afraid my car's blocking his entry to the driveway.'

'And just as well too,' Lynn retorted, horrified by the thought of Grandy discovering her on the bed with Blair.

'I've no desire for a shotgun wedding.' Blair grinned as he left the room to move his car.

'Nor any other wedding!' Lynn shouted after him, her frustration bubbling over and sending her tongue out of control. Tears blurred her eyes as she straightened her clothes and snatched at a comb, but by the time the men entered the living-room she had regained her composure.

She heard Max declare he could do with a hot drink. The remark sent her to the kitchen, and as she prepared it she heard Blair telling him that Stan had brought Delphine home. How rapidly his thoughts moved from herself to other matters, she realised sadly, then chided herself for being a fool and for allowing this fact to nag at her. Naturally, Stan and Delphine had to be on his mind.

'I shall not keep Tony home from school,' she heard him tell Max. 'Everything is to be as normal as if his mother had never been away. It'll be easier for everyone.'

He left a short time later, and as Lynn stood on the veranda watching the headlights flash along the road his words returned to haunt her mind. Everything was to be normal. And this also was normal, she thought bitterly. Blair had held her close to him. He had kissed her with a passion that told her he longed for much more. He had lifted her up into the clouds, but now she'd dropped back to earth. He had departed without a single word of love, or when they would meet again. Oh, yes— this was normal, all right.

Muttering under her breath, she told herself that her decision was obviously the correct one. It was time she went home and pushed Blair Marshall out of her system. And she'd be wise to tell Grandy at once.

Max hid his disappointment. 'I hope you'll be back soon,' was all he said, frowning slightly.

'I'll give Delphine time to settle in, and then I'll come back to see her,' Lynn promised.

'And him?'

'Him? Do you mean Stan?'

Max snorted. 'Of course I don't mean Stan. I mean *him*—the master of Marshlands.'

'Oh, *him* . . . well, that's as maybe. If he happens to be around no doubt I'll see him.' The words spoken lightly hid the ache in her heart, and again she felt there was only one course to take. She must return to her old lifestyle in which Blair did not exist.

At a later date—when she had rid herself of the longing to be with him—she would return to check up on Grandy and chat with Delphine. Perhaps she too could learn to write romance. She knew what it was like to long for

the feel of a man's arms—and she knew how it felt to
love a man who did not love her.

Lynn had been back in her father's surgery for a fortnight before she accepted the fact that life in Wellington
now held a subtle difference from the one she had known
before her recent period at Frog Hollow. Her friends
were still there, the phone rang with invitations to join
them in various activities, but somehow the parties were
flat. The men in the crowd failed to interest her, each
one being compared most unfavourably with Blair
Marshall.

Food also failed to interest her. She grew thinner and
became so listless that her parents began to regard her
pale face with anxiety until the day came when her father
spoke sternly. 'You're dieting,' he accused when she refused to leave the surgery and go to lunch.

'I am not, Daddy,' she defended. 'I'm just...not
hungry.'

'Nor do you appear to be writing,' he pointed out.

'Oh, well...I'm really waiting to hear about the last
lot I sent to the publisher,' she prevaricated.

This statement was a long way from the truth because
Lynn was not in the habit of waiting to hear the fate of
her work. Normally she set to work at once, planning
her next stories in bed, but now they evaded her while
her unruly thoughts flew to Blair Marshall. And each
night the tears trickled until she fell into a restless sleep.

Eventually the day came when she realised she must
take herself firmly in hand. She must eat more, therefore
this would be the last day she would go without lunch.
She must begin writing again and above all—she must
get Blair out of her thoughts. She must control this desperate longing to see his face.

She was alone in the surgery when she made the decision, and to force herself into work that would domi-
nate her mind she began checking the medical supplies

kept in a small room which opened behind the reception desk.

The waiting-room door opened while she was engaged in the task. A patient? she wondered. No—because surgery hours did not begin before two o'clock, therefore it must be Daddy who had returned from his routine visiting of patients.

To make sure she peeped into the waiting-room, then froze from shock. It was not her father who stood regarding her—it was Blair Marshall, suntanned, yet a little more gaunt than when she had last seen him. Confused, she wondered if the sight of him was a hallucination. She walked towards him in a daze, but got only as far as the desk, which she had to grip for support because her legs felt suddenly weak.

He stepped forward quickly. 'Are you OK? You've turned very pale...and for Pete's sake, you're as thin as a rope.'

She gave a wan smile as the sound of his voice assured her that this was no delusion. 'I'm all right. It's just that I'm a...a little surprised to see you here.' And that is the understatement of the year, she added silently to herself. Then, gathering her wits, she asked, 'Have you come to see Daddy—as a patient?'

'No. I've come to see you. You could say I've come with a special appeal.' The words were spoken in a low deep tone while his eyes raked her face anxiously.

Her gaze widened as she looked at him wordlessly. Her breath quickened and she felt the colour rising to her cheeks.

He went on, 'I'd have been here much sooner but for the sudden necessity to go to Taupo. My mother became ill and kept asking for me. She knew Stan had returned, therefore she begged me to stay longer than usual.'

'She's all right now?'

'Yes. Please try to understand why it took so long for me to come to you.'

'To—to come to me?' The words escaped as a whisper while her heart began to race.

'To tell you I love you. To ask you to marry me.'

Another silence fell upon her, and again she decided she must be dreaming. *Of course* she was dreaming. He wasn't really here at all. But it was a *nice* dream and she must be careful to stay dreaming, and to not wake up.

He moved round the end of the reception desk to stand beside her. His grip on her shoulders was real enough as he stared down into her face. 'Why are you looking at me in that dazed manner? Have you heard a single word I've said?'

'I—I think so,' she whispered, realising that this was no dream. 'It's just the shock of seeing you.'

'But you knew I'd come.'

She shook her head. 'How could I be sure?'

'Because you know I love you.'

'You never said so—therefore how could I possibly know?'

'Was your woman's intuition sound asleep?' he teased. 'Didn't my kisses tell you I love you?'

'Your kisses said plenty—but they were always followed by a disappearing act,' she was goaded to retort. 'It was as though you regretted them and wished to avoid me. A man who loved me would have been back at the crack of dawn.'

'Not this man. He had to think. He had to be sure the feelings between us had depth. You see—there was the situation between Stan and Delphine hanging over my head,' he reminded her.

'It kept rearing up to leer at you in the form of a warning?'

'Exactly.'

'But you're not Stan—and I'm not Delphine. Nor would we have their former problem.'

'I couldn't be more positive of that fact.' His arms went about her, and as he held her against him he admitted, 'The moment you left Frog Hollow I knew I couldn't live without you. And now I'm waiting for you to say the words I'm longing to hear.'

'That—I love you?' she whispered.

'Again—and louder, please.'

'Blair, I love you... I love you.' She clung to him, lifting her face for his kiss. Exhilaration filled her, sweeping away her former depression, while it seemed as if uttering the words released the tension that had previously held her emotions in check. Tears began to fill her eyes, but they were tears of joy.

'My darling.' His voice held a tremor. 'I can't even begin to tell you how much I've longed for this moment. And now I'm impatient to make you my wife.'

The words sent quivers through her, causing her arms to tighten about him as she snuggled against his shoulder.

'Tell me—how soon may that be?' The question held urgency. 'There'll be no long engagement, I trust.'

She laughed happily. 'Only long enough to plan a small church wedding with close friends and people we look upon as family, like Maisie and Bert.'

'They'll be delighted.' His lips trailed across her brow. 'Tell me more about our wedding.'

'Delphine must be my matron of honour because we really found each other through her.'

'And Stan will be my best man—that's if we can drag them down from the clouds for the occasion.' He thought for a moment then asked, 'Would you like a page boy? I can give you the name of a most willing applicant.'

'Tony? I'm glad he's with his parents and that everyone seems to be so happy.' Then a thought caused her to ask, 'Is Gary still interested in Sandra?'

'I doubt that he was ever deeply interested in the way you mean. In any case she's no longer with us. Her place has been filled by Maisie's cousin, and I've heard that Sandra has found herself a job in the South Island.'

'I'm glad she's not out of work,' Lynn admitted.

'In the meantime Gary appears to be taking notice of a farmer's daughter who lives near by. If anything comes of it I'll build another house on the property. We must have accommodation for staff if we are to be free for overseas travel.'

'Overseas travel? I don't understand.'

'Well, naturally, our Australian honeymoon won't be our only overseas trip. But that's enough for the future. There's the here and now to be considered—like the fact that I haven't kissed you for at least several minutes.'

She lifted her face. 'Such lapses must not be allowed to occur,' she whispered as her arms were raised to wind about his neck.

His head bent, and for the next few moments there was silence while his arms held her closer and his lips found hers.

But suddenly the silence was broken as the waiting-room door opened and a man's voice spoke from behind them. 'Well, well—what have we here? Is this our latest method of winning new patients? He doesn't look very ill to me.'

Lynn peeped across Blair's shoulder, her face flushed, her eyes shining with the light of happiness. Then a giggle escaped her as she said, 'Daddy—this is Blair. We're to be married. Come and meet your future son-in-law...'

Have You Ever Wondered If You Could Write A Harlequin Novel?

Here's great news—Harlequin is offering a series of cassette tapes to help you do just that. Written by Harlequin editors, these tapes give practical advice on how to make your characters—and your story—come alive. There's a tape for each contemporary romance series Harlequin publishes.

Mail order only

All sales final

- ✂ -

HARLEQUIN
Romance®

**This September, travel to England
with Harlequin Romance
FIRST CLASS title #3149,
ROSES HAVE THORNS
by Betty Neels**

It was Radolf Nauta's fault that Sarah lost her job at the hospital and was forced to look elsewhere for a living. So she wasn't particulary pleased to meet him again in a totally different environment. Not that he seemed disposed to be gracious to her: arrogant, opinionated and entirely too sure of himself, Radolf was just the sort of man Sarah disliked most. And yet, the more she saw of him, the more she found herself wondering what he really thought about her—which was stupid, because he was the last man on earth she could ever love. . . .